LADY IN

*Dee Dee
Thank you so much!*

A COLLECTION OF UTTER SPECULATION

*Happy Reading
River Eno*

LADY IN *White*

LCW Allingham   Cadence Barrett   River Eno
Melissa D. Sullivan   Susan Tulio

A COLLECTION OF UTTER SPECULATION

Copyright © 2021 LCW Allingham, Cadence Barrett, River Eno, Melissa D. Sullivan, Susan Tulio

All rights reserved. No part of this book may be reproduced or transmitted in any form or by any means, electronic or mechanical, including photocopying, recording, or by any information storage and retrieval system, without permission in writing from the author.

ISBN 978-1-946702-60-9

Cover design by Adam C. Allingham

Original Watercolor "Reflections on Alone" by Patricia Allingham Carlson

Published by Freeze Time Media

For H.A. Callum

*For your example of unrelenting
strength and optimism.
For your continued support in all the ways.*

Contents

Foreword	ix
Selene in White	1
LCW Allingham	
What the Lake Knows	43
Susan Tulio	
The Stillness of Time	83
River Eno	
Waitin' Round the Bend	117
Melissa D. Sullivan	
The Girls of Blackthorn	151
Cadence Barrett	
About the Authors	193
Acknowledgments	195

Foreword

I first heard the legend of the Lady in White on a crisp October night in 2003. I had agreed to take a lantern-lit evening tour of New Hope, an artsy and eccentric town in Bucks County, Pennsylvania.

New Hope, or "No Hope," as the sourest locals prefer to call it, has a certain reputation. People near and far know New Hope, and to a larger degree Bucks County, as a creative hub for painters, writers, and composers. It's famous for another reason: ghosts.

During the tour, three friends and I listened to our guide recite eerie stories about New Hope's paranormal past. One involved a spectral piglet taking form in a townhouse that had once been an abattoir. Another invoked the curious goings-on in a prominent inn and restaurant whose basement had been used as a morgue during the Revolutionary War. A particularly jolting story had to do with a deceased artist whose few remaining paintings hang in some of the world's most prestigious art museums; the guide swore the artist's apparition pulled her hair during a séance in a nearby home.

The most chilling story, however, began with a man speeding along a remote stretch of Bucks County road late one night. As the driver rounded a bend in the road, he saw a woman in a white gown standing on the shoulder. He swerved to avoid hitting her, and promptly pulled over to make sure she was all right. Although the woman looked elegant and proper, her attire seemed oddly anachronistic, her mood sullen. The immediate area had few, if any, homes or businesses. Realizing the woman might need help, the driver offered her a ride. She, in turn, accepted.

That's where my memory of the story gets fuzzy. I do not recall any details of the words exchanged between the driver and his peculiar passenger, but I do recall the tale's curtain line: As the driver approached the woman's destination, he looked to his right and saw nothing but an empty seat. His passenger had vanished, as if she had never entered his vehicle.

Years later, I learned that the legend of the Lady in White, or the Vanishing Hitchhiker, extends far beyond the boundaries of the region I call home. Her story has been told around the world, with versions tied to almost every country and culture. Although some of the legends are quite disturbing, as they speak to some of the darkest eras of human history, most are harmless enough. She often recounts her misfortunes, or at least alludes to them, to the individuals who offer her a ride. She almost always wears a white or light pink dress. Sometimes her dress appears wet, and the only earthly evidence of her visit after she disappears is a puddle on the passenger seat.

Who is this mysterious apparition, and why has her story been told around the world? Each version of the legend is distinct, yet they all share one commonality: tragedy.

The explanations for these ghostly figures include tortured souls whose deaths involved lost or unrequited love, suicide, or celebratory events that ended in calamity. Perhaps the Lady in White forfeited her life in a ghastly vehicular accident. Some say she drowned herself over a would-be suitor's betrayal or rejection. Or maybe she committed a grisly crime and returns to the scene as penance for her unspeakable act—a modern-day retelling of Sisyphus pushing his boulder up a mountain or Prometheus having his liver torn out by an eagle.

Of course, these legends could simply be cautionary tales to keep future generations from repeating the mistakes of their forebears. I would be surprised if one version of the legend does not have the Lady in White taking a seat in her unsuspecting victim's car, recounting her tale to the driver, and then transforming into a monstrous beast that leads the driver to his or her doom. Perhaps that's just wishful thinking on my part.

We will likely go to our graves never knowing the truth behind the legend, or even if there is any truth to be found. Each story could very well be a glorious lie, for all we know. I prefer to think we are not meant to know—not in this existence, anyway.

That's why I find books such as the one you now hold in your hands so intriguing. Humans are storytellers, and, in our stories, we strive to give purpose and meaning to the unexplainable. I consider myself fortunate to have read the two preceding "Utter Speculation" collections—the first about the Lost Colony of Roanoke, and the second about one of my favorite cryptids, the Jersey Devil. In each collection, skilled authors offer their takes on legends that have fascinated us for centuries. Their stories also give us perspectives we may not have considered previously.

The Jersey Devil collection fascinated me. Having grown up in the Philadelphia area, I had several friends who were either born in or lived in New Jersey, and nearly every one of them suggested all Garden State residents believe a hideous winged beast stalks the Pine Barrens. Prior to reading the Jersey Devil collection, I never imagined how deeply the legend might have influenced humanity in the years since the story first came into being.

You will find equally memorable tales in this collection devoted to the Lady in White. Five authors have trained their eyes on her legend. Some stories involve heartbreak, betrayal, and grief. Others pertain to love, hope, and connection—enduring principles that transcend the bounds of space and time.

After reading these tales, you might find yourself double-checking your door locks next time you drive a lonesome stretch of road late at night. Should you see a curious stranger by the side of the road, you might even be tempted to pull over and offer a ride, to learn not only what led the Lady in White to her demise, but also what draws her back from the silence of the grave.

William J. Donahue

Selene in White

LCW Allingham

They said it took Selene hours to die.

The car that hit her as she walked home, along Old Forge Road, knocked her into the woods. How many cars had passed without hearing her screams? At what point did she realize she was done? When did my sweet sister—who wanted to be an environmental attorney, who loved muscle cars and music and who always stood up for her friends—when did she give up?

She died an hour before the police found her the next morning. Her body was still warm. Her blood was still sticky.

They say there is no time limit on grief, but over twenty years later there is still a vacuum where Selene belongs. I can't move on. I am stuck.

The hole in my heart starts to scab, cushioned with the good things around me. I love my job as a third-grade teacher. I have a great little house near the beach. I grow veggies in the backyard, and sell them at the farmers market in the summer. I sing alto in the Sussex County Choir. I have friends, and an old half-deaf mutt named Waverly, who loves to run with me in the evenings. I'm content.

But I have these dreams, where I hear Selene calling for me from the woods where she died alone. When I reach her, her face is not a face. It's a hole. A black void echoing my name.

She's so angry.

No well-meaning friends or boyfriends can pull me out of that hole.

People only have so much rope to throw a person drowning in sorrow, but the depths of grief are eternal. People don't stay in my life.

Except Bob Kredich. My Bob. My BFF.

Fellow nerds in middle school, we grew up tight, with Selene tagging along behind us. He broke too when she died. Now married with two young children, he was the only person in my life who didn't tell me I needed to get over it already.

But he didn't tell me about the rumors. I found out while channel surfing late one night, after another dream. I stopped on a show called "Real Ghosts of America" as I got a bowl of ice cream. As I settled back next to Waverly on the couch, a girl was speaking on the TV, a pretty teenager who reminded me of Selene.

Her name was Katrina. She was from my hometown.

"I just, like, I saw her walking up Old Forge road, and I pulled over and asked if she needed a ride, because it's not really safe to walk along there at night. She wore this long white dress, which was weird but, like, she looked real. She got in and gave me an address and so I drove her home but when I pulled into the driveway, she wasn't in the car anymore."

The host asked, "Was the car door open?"

"No. She was just gone," Katrina said.

"And later you saw a picture?"

"Yeah." Katrina nodded, her face twisting earnestly. "I saw this picture of the girl who died from a hit and run a while back on Old Forge, and it looked just like her."

"What was the girl's name?"

"Selene Drew."

My bio mom died from a pulmonary embolism three weeks after giving birth to me. Dad married Estelle when I was two and she was pregnant. Estelle was black and I'm white. Selene was technically my half-sister, but even though her skin was darker and her hair was curly, people still mistook us for twins. Estelle was my mother in every way she was to Selene.

When Selene died, Estelle's heart broke into a million pieces and finally gave out one night. I was at college. I should have been there for her. Maybe I should have died with her.

Dad lost every woman around him. I waited for it to be my turn. I finished college. I moved away. Got a job, an apartment, a boyfriend, and then a new boyfriend. Got engaged. Broke up. Lived, aged, waiting for whatever curse he had to hit me.

Dad married again. No one else died. Not his new wife, Theresa, or her daughters. Not me. I hit thirty, thirty-five, forty. Past mom's age. Past Estelle's age.

Then I thought maybe it was me that was cursed.

My psychiatrist worked very hard on this "mystical thinking" so I didn't mention it anymore in therapy.

But I suspected I killed the women who loved me.

Dad looked very old when he opened the door to the split level on Poplar Street and ambled down the porch steps to my car to help with my bag. Waverly groaned as she stretched in the front seat and hopped out of the car.

"Hey there, kiddo," Dad said as he patted Waverly. She licked his hand and squatted to pee on the irises. "Theresa is in Cabo with her daughters. She's sorry to miss you, but maybe you'll still be here when she gets back?"

"I don't know." I hugged him and felt frail bones beneath his plaid shirt. Dad used to be beefy and solid.

We all grieve in different ways.

Theresa had redecorated again and there was a big, fake fireplace on the wall where Estelle used to hang our school pictures. On the mantle was a black and white photo in a tasteful silver frame of me and Selene on the beach. We're holding hands. I'm leading her along the shoreline, she on her chubby toddler legs, our faces turned toward the camera smiling identical smiles.

Dad caught my eye but didn't say anything. I could have asked, are you trying to let me know you haven't forgotten her? Are you trying to make sure I still feel welcome?

I let Waverly out back to get reacquainted with the yard. She peed again and settled in a patch of sunlight on the patio.

"Will Bobby be over while you're visiting?" Dad brought sandwiches to the patio table. There was an edge to his voice. Dad was always weird about Bob. He didn't think it was normal for a girl to be best friends with a boy. Or maybe he knew that there had been times when I wanted Bob to be more than a friend.

"I'm meeting him and his wife tonight," I said.

Waverly sniffed at the air as a squirrel ran past her, then flopped her head back down. I tossed her a bread crust and she sniffed that out easily enough and then came over to lick my ankle.

"Dad…" I started, not knowing how I was going to even go forward. I had considered and rejected a hundred different approaches on the drive. "Um, so I saw this show…"

"I know about the show, Brianne." He sighed heavily. "I wish they would just leave it alone."

"So, is it…true?"

Dad glowered at his half-eaten sandwich. "It's crap kids are sharing to scare themselves. And some assholes from that program decided to make a thing of it. It's an old urban legend, Brianne. They told it when I was a kid, and now they're telling it about Selene."

"What about that girl they interviewed? Katrina?"

"She's Jason Tomer's daughter."

"Jason Tomer as in…Jason I went to school with?" I recalled the high school nemesis of Bob and mine. Popular, athletic, and a total asshole who tore around town in a bright yellow Corvette like a nineties cliché.

"He lives around the corner," Dad said. "His wife died two years ago and he leaves his daughter home alone all the time. Of course, she's trying to find ways to get attention."

"Do you have his phone number?"

"Damn it, Brianne, you need to let it be. It's bad enough with kids coming by all hours of the night without you adding fuel to the fire. Let it go!"

"I can't let it go!" I shouted back. Waverly whimpered and pressed up against me, nosing the crook of my knee. I scratched under her collar to assure her I was okay.

"Selene is dead. And it was awful, but you are alive and you need to move on." Dad stood up so abruptly he knocked his chair backwards. He stormed into the house.

It was too typical of us. Dad couldn't talk and I couldn't let go. So, we fought.

I didn't know what to think of stories about Selene's ghost, but after years of being stuck here, I would grab any rope that led to my sister.

The Old Forge Tavern, at the end of Old Forge Road, wavered between historic coolness and an old pit of problems. Management changed constantly. In high school we kept tabs on how lax they were with checking IDs.

I met Bob and his awesome wife, Moira, at the tavern after a tense dinner with Dad. Bob had grown a full black beard and looked good.

"He's never been able to grow more than scruff until this year," Moira teased him.

In the familiar old building, I almost felt okay being home.

"You sure you want to give me trouble about my beard?" Bob poked the bulge of Moira's mum tum. She elbowed him, and he laughed.

She rolled her eyes at me. "You see what I put up with?"

I liked Moira. She was good to Bob, who had been through some rough times.

"You love it." Bob put his arm around Moira and pulled her to him for a kiss.

"Ug, beer breath."

"Better than wine breath," he said, rubbing his beard on her face.

"And on that note." She pulled away from him. "I need to freshen up. Back in a moment." Moira got up and Bob poked her in the butt. She swatted at him and dashed to the bathroom.

"You better be nice to her," I teasingly scolded.

"She adores me." Bob leaned forward. "You want to tell me why you're in town?"

I took a long swig of my beer.

He looked over the sparse crowd of the bar.

"You see that damned ghost show?"

"You knew?" I cried.

"I didn't want to upset you with horseshit," he said.

"No one ever wants to upset me," I said. "Don't you all realize I'm never not upset? There's no bouncing back for me."

"I know. I'm sorry." He ran a hand down his beard. "But this is just stupid shit."

"You don't believe in ghosts?" I asked.

Bob snorted. "Do you?"

"I don't know," I said.

"Aww, Bree." He took my hand. He was such a big guy now, his hand engulfed mine. I looked at it, remembering when he'd been scrawny in high school, having jerks like Jason Tomer picking on him. Jason had mercilessly bullied Bob, chipping away at him for years. After Selene, it had caught up with him and he had to leave college for a semester for intensive therapy. I didn't see him for months. When I did, he'd grown up. He'd become a new man, harder, hotter, with plenty of girlfriends to pick from. But I missed the old Bob sometimes. The sweet guy from high school who just wanted to get by.

"I'm just saying, like, if anyone had a reason to haunt it, she would," I said.

Bob settled back into his chair, taking a swig of his beer. "I still think about her every day. But these stories about ghosts walking down the road, getting rides, they're all over the world. They're urban legends. Just for the sake of argument, if Selene's ghost was around, she wouldn't settle to be some sort of cliché."

I thought of my nightmares where she called me from the woods, her face a furious black void, and I shuddered. That was how Selene would haunt.

Moira rejoined us, and I let the subject drop. I didn't want Bob to try to debunk the story. It was terrifying if it was true. But the other option was that she was just gone.

I took Old Forge Road back to my father's house. It was late, and I drove slowly, my headlights illuminating wafts of mist and the occasional flash of nocturnal eyes in the forest. No other cars were on the road and when I reached the neighborhood, I turned around and drove down again. And then again.

I saw the peeling white cross twisted with faded, faux roses placed where my sister had been hit. I stopped my car and stared at it.

It was obscured with summer growth, dirty and forgotten. I pulled onto the narrow shoulder and put on my hazard lights. It would be tragically ironic if I got hit by a car here.

The night was deafening with chirping crickets and clattering cicadas as I trudged down a shallow ditch and through the damp weeds to the cross. I strained my ears, listening for Selene's voice in the woods, for my nightmare to come true.

I would leap into the depths of hell if she called.

But as I tugged the cross from the brambles, it was only the bugs that called from the black forest along the road.

I pulled the fake flowers from the humble memorial and cleared a patch on the ground so that it would be visible from the road. People should remember.

A shriek cut through the insect chorus in the forest beside me, and I jumped back, stumbling into the ditch.

Another shriek answered from down the street, screaming women, frantic in the night.

A third scream, across the street.

No, no. Foxes. I put my hand over my chest to try and still my pounding heart and untangled myself from the weeds.

The foxes screamed at each other as I trudged back to my car, feeling like an idiot. What did I expect, coming out here in the middle of the night? With all my mystical thinking, all that was here was indifferent nature, claiming Selene's memorial, screaming in the dark.

There was a rustle in the trees as I got into my car. The damned foxes, I was sure, but I fumbled with trembling hands to shut the door and turn the key. The brush rustled again, beside my open window.

"Jerk fox," I muttered. "Jerk Bree."

As I started to pull back onto the road, my skin broke out in goosebumps and my heart started pounding again. The trees rustled harder and I floored the accelerator, shooting down the road like the devil was on my heels. My breath came hard. I was terrified and it wasn't until I reached the turn into my old neighborhood that I was able to ask myself why.

I looked in my rearview mirror but there was nothing on the dark road behind me. The fear had grabbed me so completely that it had forced me a mile down the road before I even knew what I was doing.

I should go back. I should confirm that there was nothing in the woods but foxes.

I broke out in a cold sweat at the thought.

I went home.

I dreamed, that night, of a lady in white. Her hair, eyes, skin were all white, her features shifting through many faces. She observed me from the forest, and behind her my name echoed from an angry void.

I found Katrina Tomer on social media the next day. Her profile was private with a "Fuck off" banner. I already liked her more than her douchebag dad. I sent her a DM telling her who I was and why I wanted to talk. She responded a minute later.

I'm not lying. If ur calling me a liar u can fuq off

I respected her stance.

I wrote back:

I just want to talk. I just want to know if it's really my sister.

Her reply took a half hour.

Im free l8r

She included her cell number and an emoji that I didn't try to decipher.

She accepted my friend request, and I went to her page. Katrina had changed her hair to short black spikes since the show.

Posts calling her an asshole for dragging up my sister's memory ran down her page.

HOW DO YOU THINK HER FAMILY FEELS, BITCH?!?!

There were only eighteen friends on her list. She must have purged her contacts and locked it after the backlash to her going public with her experience.

"You came home late, last night." Dad came into the kitchen. Waverly's tail started to wag, and he squatted down to give her pets and kisses.

"I'm sorry, did I wake you up?"

"I was already awake. Were you out with Bob that whole time?"

"And his wife."

"She's a nice woman. Drops off vegetables from her garden sometimes. I don't know what she sees in him."

"Bob's always stood by me."

"Except when he disappeared after Selene's funeral."

"He had a nervous breakdown. You don't know how he was bullied in school. Then to lose Selene, who was like a little sister to him…"

"But she wasn't his sister. She was yours and you needed him."

"I needed you."

Dad's face turned red, and he clenched his teeth. He rose slowly and turned away from me. "I guess we all failed."

"I gotta go," I said. I needed to get away from this conversation. I didn't want to hurt my dad, but I didn't need him harping on Bob for being a sensitive person.

I took Waverly with me to Selene's memorial, thinking maybe she and I could take a nice walk through the woods where my sister perished slowly, in horrible pain, before we met Katrina.

I found a black Honda already parked up on the shoulder.

The bumper was plastered with stickers: bands, progressive slogans, and a big one that just said "bitch." Selene would have done the same thing if she'd ever gotten that old Camaro she'd been saving for.

Waverly tugged me toward Selene's cross, where the ground was disturbed.

"I planted Maltese Cross seeds," a girl said. I looked up to Katrina, cloaked in forest shadows. "They're red and they grow really well. People will notice them when they bloom."

"Thank you," I said.

She squinted at me. "You look like Selene."

"I'm Bree," I said. "People sometimes thought we were twins."

"My dad doesn't like you."

I smiled, tightly. "Your dad was a dickhead in high school."

"He still is," she said, and stepped out into the sunlight.

Katrina Tomer had the same kind of attitude as my sister.

The way she walked with her shoulders back, swaying a bit, her stance was always on guard. I thought of Selene as my sweet sister, but she wasn't afraid to speak her mind, stand up for herself and others. She organized a sit-in when the school sent a girl home for wearing a baby tee. Like Selene, I bet Katrina Tomer didn't take any shit.

Maybe that was why Selene had come to her.

"What a sweet girl," Katrina cooed, reaching carefully for Waverly to scratch her ears.

Waverly rolled onto her back, her pink tongue lolling as she grunted with joy.

Katrina kept her eyes on Waverly as she spoke. "I've seen her five times. The first time I was with my friend…my ex-friend, Maddie. She had loose, curly hair and she wore this real long white dress. I pulled over to see if she needed help and she said she needed a ride home. Then she wasn't in the car when we pulled into the driveway. Your dad came out and we told him what happened and he just told us to go home. Maddie denies it now. The next time, I was alone when I saw her, and I asked her what happened 'cause, like, I didn't know she wasn't a real person. She just said the same thing. The same thing happened but this time your dad got upset and told me to stop coming around."

I worried my lower lip. Selene hadn't been wearing a white dress when she died. She'd been wearing low-rise, wide-leg jeans and a green halter top. And her hair had been pulled up in a tight bun.

"So how come you're white and your sister was black?" Katrina asked quietly, seeming unsure it was an appropriate question.

"Different moms," I said. "Did you tell your dad about it?"

"My dad works all the time," she said. "He won't even talk to me about the show stuff even though he signed the papers allowing me to do it. My mom died a couple years ago and he doesn't deal with it, so he works, and I take care of myself."

"I'm sorry," I said. "My mom died too. Both of them."

"And your sister." She gave Waverly one final pat and then stood up. "That sucks."

"Did you pick her up again?"

"I was mad after that second time so when I saw her again, like a month later, I just pulled over and was like, 'I'm not giving you a ride this time,' and she didn't say anything. And I felt like shit about it. So then, the next time I picked her up, but I tried to get her to talk to me. She just stared. She had these really weird eyes, like they were just blank and the only thing she said is 'I want to go home.' I tried to watch her the whole time. She was still in the car when I pulled onto the street and when I started to turn into the driveway but I had to, like, look to get into the driveway and then she wasn't there anymore. I started to hear that other people had seen her too. Like other kids in my school, and Maddie was telling everyone about it, and we set up a message board about it where people were posting their experiences."

"Is the board still active?" I asked.

"I took it down, but I have the archives. When that show did the episode on her, they interviewed a lot of people, but they used a lot of my interview, because I'd seen her the most. I didn't think it was bad but people got upset, and everyone else just backed away. Now everyone hates me. I wasn't trying to make trouble. I even…look…"

She opened up her pictures on her phone, where she had shots of official looking documents. "I even got the police records and have been trying to, like, figure out what happened. Did you know they found skin under her nails?"

"The police said it wasn't related," I said. "She was hit by a car. They thought she got in a fight with her friends. That's probably why she was walking home. They never matched it."

"Did she scratch her friends a lot?" Katrina asked, with a skeptically raised brow.

It had never sat well with me either.

"The last time I saw her was different." Katrina's voice trembled. Waverly nosed her and Katrina pet her absently. "It was after the show aired the first time.

"I had just had, like, a really bad night. Lost most of my friends. And whatever, they sucked anyway if they would turn on me that quick. But I was upset driving home, and I saw her walking from behind, the same as always, and I pulled up alongside of her. I dunno if I was going to yell at her or give her a ride or just ask what was going on, but when she turned toward me it wasn't her the way I saw her before."

"What do you mean?" I asked.

Katrina tugged at her spiked hair. "Her face—it wasn't there. Instead of her face there was just—just this hole. This sucking black hole."

There was a strange consistency to the reports that Katrina had collected. Selene was only seen on Thursday and Friday nights, between ten p.m. and midnight.

All the reports described Selene as looking the way Katrina said, her hair loose and long, wearing a long, white dress, pale but solid, not ghostly.

"Did you ever touch her?" I asked.

"Never," Katrina said. "Like, I wouldn't just touch some girl I don't know. That would be rude."

I remembered Katrina's father grabbing a handful of my ass during a track meet and smirking. "Keep running, Drew. You'll get there."

He was the worst.

"Do you think she looked like that because she was mad at me, about the show?" Katrina asked.

"I don't think so," I said. "Would you be willing to look for her with me? Thursday?"

"If I can help you with this—I want to. I just— it was really scary the last time."

"You don't have to do anything you don't want. You don't owe me anything. I shouldn't even ask."

"No, please don't say that. I know adults have, like, these rules and stuff. But I feel like Selene chose me for a reason and I want to help her. I lost someone too."

Dad took to Waverly like she was a grandchild, encouraging her up onto his lap while he watched TV and feeding her treats when he thought I wasn't looking.

He made roast chicken with mashed potatoes for dinner. Afterwards, he picked the carcass and made a special platter for Waverly, assuring me that it would be good for her.

I tried to tell him about Katrina but he changed the subject back to Waverly, asking if I had taken her to any specialists for her eyesight loss.

Bob came to my rescue.

When he came to the door, Dad's face darkened.

"Hello, Mr. Drew." Bob stuck out his hand.

Dad grunted, giving Bob's hand a brief shake, then coaxed Waverly outside with him.

"Some things never change, huh?" Bob said after he went.

"We're not getting along," I said. "Don't take it personally."

I told him about Katrina as we got into his car.

"God, that's karma for you. Jason Tomer ending up with a freak for a daughter."

"Nah, she's a really cool kid."

"She's telling people she's picking up a hitchhiking ghost, Bree. You're not buying her bullshit, right? She's Jason's kid, for Christ's sake."

I bristled, protective of the girl. "Never mind."

"Wait, are you mad at me?"

"I said, never mind. Where are we going?"

"The Old Forge Tavern," Bob grumbled.

"But that's the other way down the road," I said.

"I'm taking the scenic route."

"The scenic route is fifteen minutes. Old Forge Road leads right to the tavern."

"I don't like to go that way, Bree. Okay? It makes me...It brings back all those memories."

I remembered Selene comforting Bob after he'd failed to make the basketball team once again. I remembered how bad he looked at her funeral. Everyone grieves differently.

I sighed. "So, what's changed since I was last in town?"

"There are now two Wawas."

"Now that's the excitement I've been looking for."

There were some old friends at the Old Forge Tavern, and Bob and I were good once we dropped the ghost subject, but I got tired of all the noise and commotion. People I'd known all my life, who knew me, my family, our story, danced around it like it was fire that would burn them. I got a lot of light hugs and hand pats and "Oh good for you!" about my very ordinary single life as a teacher near the beach with a dog.

It felt forced. The conversation was loud and shallow to cover up the traumas of our pasts. Even Bob, talking the loudest, laughing the hardest, hid the scars of Selene's death and a childhood of being bullied by assholes like Jason.

I retreated to the bathroom when it became too much, regretting my decision to escape from my dad's weird home dynamic to this weird dynamic.

At the antique sink I let cold water run over my hands.

As I tried to center myself, something moved behind me, brushing my shoulder. I looked around and saw a blur of white move through the door. I broke out in chills.

I turned back to the spotty old mirror, and the face that looked back was not mine.

The skin was darker, the black hair pulled back tight. I gasped as it moved closer, squinting at the reflection.

"Selene?" I whispered.

She scrunched her nose and pulled the tie out of her hair, letting it fall loose in bouncing curls around her shoulders. She turned her face from side to side, examining it in the mirror.

She was so, so young and so, so beautiful.

"Selene," I said again, tapping on the glass. She stopped and looked around her.

"Bree?" she whispered.

"Selene!" I cried, but she shook her head and turned away. She walked to the door behind me, looking around the room once more, then she walked out.

My own reflection was back, wild-eyed, haggard and so old compared to my fresh and beautiful young sister.

What had I just seen?

Selene, wearing what she wore her last night, in this mirror. She'd gone out in a green halter top, with her hair tied up. She'd supposedly gone to her friend's house.

A small, pained cry echoed through the bathroom and it took a second to realize it was mine. I trembled, gasping. It couldn't be. Yet I'd never had a hallucination. It could only be a vision of Selene, here the night she died.

And the vision had heard me back.

Dad was in a mood Thursday, crashing around in the kitchen when I wandered downstairs late that morning. Waverly chewed on a raw hide in the corner, looking back and forth at us.

"Is something wrong?" I asked.

"I can't find Estelle's cast iron pan," he cried, as if it were an emergency.

"Maybe Theresa packed it away."

"You always assume the worst of her."

"I barely know her."

"Well, you should try. She's a great mother."

"I'm not trying to fill Estelle's place. That's what you do!"

He stopped his furious search, his face reddening. "What does that mean?"

"You don't deal with your loss. You replace it. You replaced mom with Estelle, Estelle and Selene with Theresa and her daughters. If I die, you'll replace me. You pretend they were never even here. But I can't do that. I'll never get over it and no one can replace them!"

I stormed to my room and slammed the door, feeling like a defiant teenager. Waverly scratched on my door, and I let her in. She hopped up on my bed, and I snuggled my face into her fur.

After a while, my dad knocked.

"Bree?"

I didn't answer. Waverly licked my face.

Dad came in and slumped onto the end of the bed. I waited to fight with him some more.

"I should have told you about the ghost stories," he said.

I sat up and Waverly wagged her tail, thankful for the shift in my despondency.

"Yes," I said. "You should have."

He buried his face in his hands. "Selene had a boyfriend. She said she was going out with her friends that night, when you said you were staying in to study. Estelle had that rule about meeting boyfriends at a proper dinner, but I thought she was too strict. You skated around that rule all the time with Bobby."

"I was never dating Bob," I interjected.

"But you liked him."

I sank back into my bed.

"Estelle went to bed early with a migraine. You were locked in your room studying. Selene got picked up by some loud hot-rod car none of her friends drove. You know how she always loved loud cars. I heard that car a lot that year."

"You don't know who he was?" I asked.

Dad shook his head. "When they did the autopsy, she had alcohol in her system. She had a fake ID on her. The police said they knew who she was out with but he had an alibi. They wouldn't tell me who. I think someone paid to keep it quiet."

"But he could have been the one to hit her!" I said.

"If they had a fight and she was walking home alone—"

"All evidence pointed to an accident."

"But the tissue under her nails—"

"It wasn't him."

"It sounds like a cover up!"

"There's more, Bree," Dad said, before I could go down that rabbit hole. "Estelle didn't just die of grief. She stopped breathing in her sleep. She was mixing pills with wine, just trying to cope. I knew and I didn't—"

Dad started to shudder and buried his face deeper into his hands. For a moment everything was silent and then a great, gasping wail escaped him.

"It's all my fault, Bree. I let them all go and I didn't do anything to save them. Every one of them. I was at work when your mother died and you were just a tiny thing, alone with her all day. I let Selene go off with some boy to a bar. And then I let Estelle fall into oblivion. And when we needed to come together, I left you blowing in the wind. You're strong, Bree. You've endured, but it was my failings that you endured."

"No," I burst out. "It's not your fault! It's mine. I should have been with her that night. I wasn't studying. I was waiting for a boy to call. A stupid boy. I bailed on her for nothing!"

"Oh, sweetheart." Dad clutched me tight to him and we cried together. "It's not your fault. None of it. Not at all."

Dad sucked at grief. But at least now I understood. In the only way he knew how, he had been trying to care for me. He loved me, and he loved Selene.

I think that was all I had ever really needed to know from him. That the women in his life weren't replaceable. That if I died, the space I occupied in his heart wouldn't be filled in with a surrogate.

It was enough to know that, after all this time. Enough for now.

Katrina's car was alone in the newly paved driveway of the immaculate colonial around the corner from my father's home. The house was well kept, bland and sterile.

A flickering porch light came on as I pulled up. Its sickly yellow illumination barely penetrated the gloom gathered around her house as Katrina shuffled out to my car. She carried a ratty backpack, scribbled with white out pen and pinned with political patches.

"Thanks for picking me up early," she said. "My dad's flight is coming in and I'd rather not be home when he gets here."

"Won't he be worried?" I asked.

She shrugged. "He probably won't notice."

I felt an unexpected stab of pity for Jason Tomer, former high school bully and current widower/single father who couldn't relate to or understand his brilliantly weird teenage daughter.

We went for a late dinner outside of town, then headed back to Old Forge Road around ten. We looped up and down for a while, looking for Selene on every pass, before pulling over to the shoulder, near her memorial.

The night was muggy but not too hot so we opened the windows and listened to the crickets chirping. We talked about Katrina's future plans. She wanted to be a marine biologist.

"There's this documentary about this lady who removes fish hooks from sharks," Katrina said, "and I feel like if I could do something like that, I would be happy. Is that terrible? That I could be happy even though my mom is gone?"

"No. It's how it's supposed to be. Your mom would want you to." Everyone grieves differently, and people are supposed to move on. Just not me. Not yet.

A fox shrieked in the forest. We both jumped, and then giggled.

"When I heard them the other night, I almost shit my pants," I said.

Katrina giggled harder. A car drove past, the first in a while, and we settled into silence. I looked at my phone.

"Eleven-thirty," I said. "We should head home soon."

The brush rustled beside the car and a cool breeze blew through the windows. We both shivered.

"Let's loop around for one more pass," she suggested.

"That happened when I stopped here before," I whispered.

"Pull away," she hissed.

I turned on the car and the brush rustled again. My skin broke out in goosebumps, and I gunned the car back out onto the road.

"Okay, turn around," Katrina said after we went a few hundred feet, but my foot seemed glued to the gas. She touched my arm. "Bree?"

I pulled over, panting.

"Are you okay?" she asked.

I felt weird, a chilly tingle scraping over my skin. "Maybe you should drive."

I traded seats with her, and she turned the car around.

All the hair on my skin stood up straight. Katrina rolled down the road and as we passed the memorial, we saw her.

Selene, in white, glided up the street, sliding in and out of the black shadows of the forest. Katrina drove past her and turned the car around. My heart beat like a bass drum, pulsing in my ears. I wanted to be elated but I only felt dread.

The headlights caught her curls bouncing off her narrow shoulders. The tattered skirt of her long white dress swayed behind her.

Katrina pulled up alongside of her. "Hey," she said, her casual tone indicating she didn't feel the same terror as me.

Selene looked at us, her big brown eyes blank. "I want to go home."

"Hop in," Katrina said.

Sirens clanged in my head.

Selene opened the back door and slid in.

I forced myself to turn around. It was like running in a dream, my motions painfully slow, until at last I faced her.

I stared at the thing in the back seat. It stared blankly past me.

"You're not Selene," I said with certainty.

Its eyes flicked to me. The irises melted away into whiteness. Color faded from its skin and hair and its features began to shift, the nose widening, narrowing, the lips full then thin. I choked. It grabbed my hand. Its grip was ice cold and terrible. I reached for Katrina and saw she was frozen, her face partially turned toward me, her eyes locked somewhere in time. I finally screamed and the thing posing as Selene leaned in closer.

It was the thing I had dreamed of that first night home, with Selene's angry echo behind it. "What are you? Where is my sister?" I cried.

The thing blinked rapidly several times and then released my hand. I slammed back into the dashboard, and fumbled to open the car door. When it finally swung open, I meant to run, but before I could get out of the car, I pitched forward and threw up onto the street.

"She calls for you," the thing said when I gasped for air. "When she awakens, she goes to you. Do you hear when she calls?"

"What?" I struggled to comprehend that this was happening, yet could not deny it.

"Selene," it said. "She and you are tightly bonded. You know this."

"What have you done with her?"

"I keep her," it said. "I keep so many. I try to get them home. Sometimes they cannot be kept. Mary goes to the dance hall. Lydia goes to the bridge. Selene goes to you when she wakes."

"What?"

"She is such fury." It used my sister's voice, but the inflection was wrong. It spoke like someone much older than Selene had ever been. "She seeks you. She seeks vengeance. She has tied these things together."

My fingers clutched my seat so hard they ached.

"I found her raging spirit and eased her to sleep. I try to take her home. That is what I can do."

"You help her?" I asked.

The thing's face shifted back to that of Selene's. "It is my task to take these shattered girls. I succeed sometimes, but I forget the way so easily."

"What are you?"

"The White Lady," it said. "I have many other names, but none of them are mine. I take in my wards. I help them sleep. I seek peace for them. They are so angry. Once I was angry. It was long ago. This is my purpose now and they feed me well."

"Feed you?"

"Their fury, your fear. I do not hurt. Never hurt. They are beyond hurt. I find them peace so they can pass on."

"Selene cannot pass on?"

"Some pass when I can get them home. Some pass after a long rest. Selene wakes often and she is never subdued. She searches for you. And you search for her. This is different. You are both different. Why do you seek each other?"

"Because … it's my fault."

"No, no." It shook its head and Selene's curls bobbed around its face. "But it is someone's fault."

"Do you know who hit her?"

It cocked its head to the side like an animal, listening to a sound only it could hear. "I must go."

It vanished, as if it had never been there.

Katrina gasped beside me, staring at the empty seat.

I couldn't find the words to explain. I took over the wheel and drove her home.

There was another car in Katrina's driveway and a shadow standing beneath the sickly yellow porchlight as I pulled in.

"Shit, Dad's waiting for me," Katrina muttered. "Just pull away quick or he'll—"

It was too late. Jason Tomer lumbered toward my car.

Katrina hopped out, struggling with her backpack, and dashed past him for the door.

"I told you to be home by eleven," he snapped and knocked on my window.

"Hi, Jason," I said, rolling it down.

He stumbled back a few steps when he saw me.

"Bree Drew," I said. "We went to school together. Katrina has been helping me out with a project. I'm sorry. I didn't know she had a curfew."

"Bree," Jason murmured. "Bree Drew."

"Jesus, Dad, you look like you're going to be sick," Katrina said.

"I'll talk to you in the morning," Jason barked.

"Whatever." Katrina gave me a wave before she went inside.

"Bree," Jason said for the third time and I realized that he had thought he'd seen someone else when he looked into my car.

The revelation hit.

"You knew Selene," I said.

"Shit," Jason said. "Yeah, I did. You want to come in for a drink?"

Jason had been her boyfriend with a loud car. Bullying, loud, arrogant, sexist Jason. Of course she couldn't tell me.

"It's your fault," I hissed.

He gave a defeated nod and walked inside. I followed him, buzzing with fury.

Grief had etched deep lines around my mouth and eyes. Some days I looked into the mirror and wondered how I could look so old.

Jason looked worse.

His formerly handsome face was puffy and red. He had bags under his eyes, chipmunk cheeks and a gray, receding hairline. It was hard to believe he was the same age as Bob who had only grown more attractive.

Jason unlocked a cabinet in the dusty living room and pulled out a bottle of expensive vodka and two tumblers. He poured two glasses and handed me one.

I sipped it and he threw his back and poured another.

"So, uh, how you been?" he asked.

"I don't want to make small talk, Jason." I paced the dusty beige carpet. "What happened to my sister that night?"

"I met her at our graduation ceremony," he said.

"She was checking out my Corvette. And we fell for each other."

I wanted to lunge, to wrap my hands around his puffy throat, but a powerful wave of nausea hit me and I stumbled back into a faded recliner. Jason raised his hands.

"I swear to God, I loved her. She was funny and beautiful and tough."

"I know why you would love her! Why would she give a shit about you?"

"I think it was just the car, at first. She loved cars, but she didn't care about the popularity stuff. That was so…cool. I fell hard. But she drove me crazy too. That night we were at the Old Forge Tavern and she got mad and left."

"And you let her?" I cried.

"Selene did what she wanted," he said. "I chased after her, I tried to get her to come back, to let me give her a ride home. She slapped me and stormed off. And yeah, I let her. I was mad too."

"What a prince."

"I regret it every day. I was an asshole, but she wouldn't even tell her family about me because you hated me so much."

"You grabbed my ass and relentlessly bullied Bob Kredich."

Jason frowned, and his eyes got distant, like this was news to him. Did he really not know how awful he was?

"Why didn't you tell the police you were with her that night?" I demanded.

"I did! I went to the station as soon as I found out. But my uncle was on the force. He asked that it be kept off the report. Since I obviously hadn't been the one to hit her."

"It's not obvious to me. You were mad at her. You were drinking. You drove like an asshole."

"I was at the tavern all night after she left, drinking with my friends. Everyone saw us."

"But somehow no one saw Selene?"

"She was only there with me for a few minutes. She talked to that guy, your friend. She went to the bathroom. She came out and started on me, calling me a jerk. I said she was just trying to sound like you. Then she stormed out."

"She talked to *my* friend?"

"Yeah, that skinny guy you mentioned. Bob."

My pulse throbbed in my face. The world dropped out around me. My vision twisted into a hollow tunnel, and I could only see Jason Tomer's perplexed, old face and hear the rush of blood in my ears.

"Bob wasn't there," I insisted.

"I forgot about it, but yeah he was. He left early too. He was always hanging around Selene while we were dating. Always pulling her off. I tried to fight him once, but she told me to back off and I did. I wasn't a monster. I tried to be respectful of her. I tried to be better for her."

I barely heard him. My mind spun over and over the possibility that Bob was there that night. That he knew she was dating Jason Tomer. That he saw her at the bar. That he left around the same time as her.

And he never told anyone.

I spent the next day curled up with Waverly on the old couch in the family room. Selene and I had shared this couch, watching car shows and late-night TV, eating popcorn, talking about life. I was surprised Theresa hadn't replaced it, but glad. The couch felt like a life raft in a wild and unfamiliar ocean.

Dad came in for a bit, even put a tentative arm around me. He didn't know how my grief had grown to dread in the last day.

At dark, I left the house on foot, walking out of the neighborhood and down Old Forge Road. It was Friday night and traffic was typical. I walked in the run-off ditch, my jeans soaking up the dampness of the grass.

I sat next to Selene's memorial. I listened to the foxes. I waited for the thing to come for me. I knew it would.

First Katrina came, parking her car on the shoulder. "Are you okay?" she asked.

"Are you?" I deflected.

She jumped across the ditch to sit down beside me. "It's a lot. My dad—I can't believe he didn't tell me! When I told him I saw her, he just yelled. Made me feel like I did something wrong."

"Everyone grieves differently," I said.

"I guess we never know the people we love." She put her hand on my shoulder.

"I bailed on Selene that night, because I was waiting

for a boy to call," I whispered. "I was going to ask him out. It was Bob."

Katrina didn't respond. Her hand remained, still, on my shoulder, and I turned to see she was again petrified, her mouth slightly open, tears quivering on her cheeks.

"Your sister is awake." The Lady in White slid out of the woods beside me, its pale face shifting, her eyes glowing. "She calls for you."

Dread clenched my chest. I slid out from under Katrina's hand and followed the lady into the forest. The night was silent, the crickets locked in between time. The foxes frozen between their screams. The damp summer air felt thick as I trailed behind the lady, through the brambles, past the old, twisted trees. I could barely see in the shadowed darkness, but a weight bore down on me with every step, pressing heavier as the woods closed around us. I heard the screams, hollow echoes, as if coming through a mile-long tunnel. I had stepped into my nightmare. I took a deep breath and pushed forward until the faint haze of the lady stopped beneath a massive oak.

"Selene, your sister is here," it whispered and the echo got louder. My vision adjusted, and I saw a shadow crouched at its feet. Jeans and a halter top, black hair pulled back tight, and where her face should have been, a cavity, a well of despair, and from it, her voice, screaming my name.

I fell to my knees. "Selene," I wept. "I am so sorry. I'm here. I'm here for you."

The screams intensified, and I looked into the vacuum. It pulled at me, and I leaned in, my heart pounding, terror raking down my back. This was my sister, back with me at last.

I let myself fall into the void of her fury.

Everything hurt.

"Selene, get in."

Bob pulled up on the shoulder of the empty road and leaned out the window of his dented junker, his brow furrowed.

"It's fine. I need to walk it off," I replied. My voice wasn't mine. It was younger, and husky with tears. None of this was mine. I wasn't me. But I was. I was Selene. Of course I was. Who else would I be?

"C'mon. Your sister would kill me if she knew I let you walk home alone."

"You're not going to tell her—"

"No way." Bob raised his hands. "Unless you insist on walking."

I was irritated. Bob was always playing these games, pushing in where he didn't belong. But I didn't exactly love the idea of walking. I was already feeling stupid about the fight with Jason. I got into Bob's car.

He didn't go. He reached his arm around me and pulled me close to him. I stiffened. I hated when guys did this.

"I'm sorry he's such a jerk, Selene," he said, kissing my temple. He smelled like whisky. I broke out in goosebumps, my skin itching. Maybe I should just walk.

"It's fine," I said, tugging away from him. He didn't take the hint, holding me tighter.

"You don't have to put up with that shit," Bob said, unwinding the band from my hair as he held me. "You can get a nice guy. Lots of nice guys like you."

"Yeah, I know," I said, finally pushing back from him. "I just want to go home right now, okay?"

He reached out and twisted one of my curls around his finger. "Bree's always been jealous of your hair. Black girls have such soft hair."

"Bob, cut it out," I said, sweeping my hair back. He held to the strand and gave it a yank.

"I'm just looking out for you," he said. "Haven't I always looked out for you?"

"I can get some time in with Bree before she goes back to school if I get home now. I never should have gone out tonight."

"Bree's fine," he said, finally releasing my strand. "Just talk to me for a little bit."

He ran his finger down my face and I pulled away and tried to tie my hair back again. He grabbed my hair tie from my fingers, grinning like it was all some fun game.

"Forget it," I said, and opened the car door to leave. Bob grabbed my wrist, tightly.

"C'mon. Stop being such a bitch."

"Let the fuck go of me," I barked, yanking from his grip.

He reached for me again and I lashed at him, raking

my nails down his arm. He jerked back and I got out and slammed the door. I started back up the street, seething. Bob went too far this time.

"I thought you were different than other girls," he called. "But you're just another slut, spreading for big jocks with nice cars."

"And you're the pathetic loser everyone thinks you are. Someday Bree will figure it out too," I shot back.

Bob's car screeched up beside me. His face was purple. "If Bree had any idea that her precious baby sister was just another whore, she would kick your stupid ass all the way to the projects, you ghetto bitch."

I saw red.

His tires squealed on the asphalt for a second before shooting forward. I grabbed a chunk of macadam from the crumbling edge of the road and chucked it, hard. It nailed the trunk of his car and he screeched to a halt.

Bob stuck his head out the car window. I thrust up my middle fingers and waved them. He swung his car around. I saw his eyes, wild, feral. Furious. Then just the white of the headlights.

I had made a mistake.

I leapt as the car roared toward me, but too late. The impact shattered me from the bottom up and propelled me into an oak tree in the black forest. Bob's junker screeched down the road, taking the light, leaving me broken in the darkness.

It felt like an eternity, the pain and the blackness, and the anger boiling into rage, for that boy, for the world, most of all for myself, until I soaked in it.

An eternity, until I saw the hand, the face. Her face. My face.

Brianne. My Brianne. "I love you, Selene…"

We became one, and she lifted me up.

I clutched the shade of Selene in my arms. It felt like a bundle of spiderwebs. A creeping chill ran up my arms, gripping my insides and twisting through them. The Lady in White walked beside me as we trudged up Old Forge Road, toward home.

The screaming had stopped.

I didn't know how I got here.

Once I had fallen into the void, I had been somewhere else. Someone else. I remembered that, the pain, the disgust. The fury.

The world remained still. Ahead of us a frozen car cast beams of light and I walked through them, clinging to the bundle of my sister. The echo of abyss was fainter now, but I did not look at her, afraid she would vanish into mist in my arms. The Lady disappeared in the light and emerged again in the darkness behind the car.

My feet squished in my wet shoes. When I turned into our neighborhood, Selene shifted in my arms, and a cool hand held to my neck. I walked to my father's house, our house, where we had been so tightly wound to each other.

We had kept secrets from each other. They had frayed our bond but not broken it. We were here now, she and I.

As I approached the driveway, she wrapped her phantom arms around my neck and her legs around my waist. She rested her head against my shoulder. I carried her as if she were my child, like I did when she was so small and I was her big sister who always protected her.

I held her tight and whispered, "We're almost home, Selene. Almost home."

The whistling emptiness was now a sighing breeze. The Lady stopped at the end of the driveway.

"This is where I tried to take her. But it was you, Brianne. You are the home she sought."

The Lady faded into the night as I opened the door to our house. Selene's ghostly fingers gripped my back and we crossed the threshold together.

Selene remained.

I carried her up the stairs.

No one ever renovated Selene's room. I set her down on her black and pink zebra comforter. Her fingers released me and her face, her real face, looked around at her yellowed *Destiny's Child* poster, the chipped white desk and the matching dresser. The space frozen in time, waiting for her return. She smiled at me, young and beautiful and sweet and fierce.

"I love you, Bree," she said.

"I love you. I'm so sorry."

"I never blamed you."

"But I—"

"Shhh." A sweet voice spoke beside me and I looked up to see Estelle bathed in light. "My sweet girls. Let go."

She kissed my cheek and reached down to take Selene's hand.

They were gone in an instant, but the room glowed in gold. A sob bubbled up from the oldest, darkest pit of my heart and wailed into the night, shattering all the walls I'd built to contain my grief. Time started again. Dad came in and hugged me tight and his grief overflowed as well, at last. Waverly pushed between us, kissing our teary faces.

When our tears were done at last, the first gold beams of morning light illuminated the horizon.

I called the police.

Selene was at peace, and maybe someday I could be too.

But first I would have justice.

It was late September and Ryan and his best friend, Talia, had just left the movie theater. Talia's grandmother was driving and they were traveling on N. Tatum Blvd. on a two mile stretch of desert about ten minutes north of Scottsdale.

The night was warm and the dark skies were littered with stars. Lights blurred in the distance. Rocks and cacti dotted the dry landscape. But there was something else. A woman walked on the side of the road. She looked disheveled: wild hair, white nightgown, shaking her head back and forth. She pulled a suitcase behind her.

It happened so fast that they didn't think to stop because by the time they processed what they had seen they had driven on. They looked behind but couldn't see her. She either disappeared or walked off the road and into the desert area.

-Cave Creek, Arizona 2013

What the Lake Knows

Susan Tulio

A fiery streak blazed across the sky. Clouds stretched long by the wind turned red, then pink, then purple. Dusk settled on Grand Haven as the sun made its descent through the trees.

Traffic snarled as a few tourists pulled to the side of the road to view the last of the day as it slipped into Lake Michigan. Chase Andrews flipped the car's sun visor back up, his thumb catching the clip that held Peyton's picture and the note she'd left behind.

He pulled the once-white card from the clasp. A green weeping willow was printed on the front, its branches bending gracefully toward the outer edges. Instead of a favorite flower, Peyton had a tree. It graced her business cards, travel cup, and even a drunken attempt at artwork from one of those painting parties.

The canvas and favorite coffee mug came with Chase when he packed up their home. The rest of her things he had donated.

Ahead, a brightly lit Ferris wheel spun slowly. Red taillights flashed in gridlock. He hesitated before opening the card. The sweet sound of Peyton's voice drifted through Chase's head as if Peyton were reading the words out loud.

Chase,

Happy fifth anniversary. It seems like just yesterday that we got married. I can't imagine navigating through my hectic life without you. You soothe me, especially when I've been running around like a crazy person all day. You're all I've ever wanted. And each day I fall more in love with you.

Yours Forever,

Peyton

P.S. I know you haven't seen the lake house since closing, but I'm glad you let me manage the renovations myself. I can't wait to show you.

Chase thought back to that morning a year ago. The mattress had dipped as Peyton slipped from the warm sheets. He'd reached out to pull her back, but she wriggled from his grasp and padded toward the bathroom.

"Get showered. Let's go out for breakfast when I get back," Peyton said.

She blew him a kiss as she left, eager to catch the sunrise on her morning run. Her golden ponytail bounced behind her. It was the last glimpse he would have of her alive.

An hour later, Chase raced to the ER in a daze. He ran for the triage desk. A staff member pulled him aside and led him to a private conference room.

"Your wife suffered a heart attack." Chase felt the doctor's hand on his arm. "I'm sorry. It was fatal. Son? Do you understand?"

Chase couldn't even begin to understand. He had stared at the doctor in disbelief as a dark, sickening grief filled his heart.

Chase pulled himself out of the pain and into the now. Carnival lights spun dizzily. The wind carried the smell of barbecue, corn dogs and French fries. Chase inched his SUV past the crowds. Finally, nothing but open road on Lake Shore Drive.

Cedar, spruce and pine trees hedged in the two-lane highway with only a dusky stripe peeking through. Streetlights blazed their golden hue through the darkness as a small town took shape.

A woman walked barefoot, sopping wet, on the side of the road. Her white dress clung to her skin like she'd just emerged from the water.

Chase tapped the brakes. The SUV's high beams cut right through her.

"Hey, are you all right?" Chase stopped the car. "Do you need help?"

She looked straight at him, but it was like looking through a veil.

A car swerved around him, the driver yelled and Chase pulled onto the shoulder. He threw the SUV into park, got out and circled around. But she was gone. The lady had vanished into thin air.

"Hello! Do you need help?" Chase called out toward the scrub of trees. Nothing except the near deafening sound of crickets. He hoped she wasn't afraid. More so, he hoped she wasn't hurt.

Another driver rudely laid on the horn as they sped past. Was it a mistake selling everything and moving here? He needed a new start. A place where he could avoid the concerned glances from his family and friends. It was uncomfortable knowing that people were watching him for signs that he was still grieving or depressed.

Chase sat back in the driver's seat and waited in case the woman appeared. After five minutes, he gave up and drove on.

Gift shops and beachside cafes dotted the main drag. Chase pulled into a Quik Stop for gas and a few groceries. He roamed the aisles, loading his arms and then juggled it all to the checkout counter.

"Sorry, dude, I didn't see you waiting." A twenty-something clerk with a mop of sandy-brown hair and a lazy smile walked toward the cash register. "I was in back for a sec." The guy reeked of weed and Chase couldn't help but smile.

"Is that your Jeep Cherokee at the pump?" the clerk asked.

"Yeah."

"Is that a Hacker-Craft you're towing? What year is she?"

"'63 Sportabout," Chase answered with a smile.

"Dude, that boat's extra!"

Chase laughed. "It needs a ton of work. I picked it up cheap at an auction. By the way, I'm looking for Evergreen Drive. Is it around here somewhere?"

"You the guy that bought Evelyn and Walter's old place?"

Chase nodded.

"Sad, how Evelyn died. Did you hear the story?"

"No, I didn't."

"She was kind of like the social mayor around here. She collapsed at the Coast Guard festival two years ago. Went down like a ton of bricks. I was working the beer stand and saw the whole thing. Turned out she had a massive brain tumor. My friend's mom, who's a nurse, said she couldn't walk, or talk, couldn't do anything but lie in a hospital bed. She was a vegetable for months. After she died, her husband, the congressman, who they say was a pretty strange man, moved to one of those fancy older communities."

"I had no idea. Why was the congressman strange?"

"I dunno. He just had a bad temper. Was seen screaming at his wife a bunch of times at the country club."

"I see. We only dealt with lawyers and real estate brokers when we bought the house."

"There was some hottie who used to oversee the work being done. She liked to stop in here for sweet tea. Was that your wife?" he asked. "No disrespect." He placed the last of the groceries in a bag. "That'll be ninety-two sixty-one for the gas and the grub."

Chase felt like he'd taken a punch to the gut. His stomach clenched with a sick feeling of emptiness. The air grew heavy, making it hard to breathe. He looked around the store trying to picture Peyton roaming the aisles. He buried his hands into his pockets and inhaled deeply, swallowing his grief. It had only been a year, but he thought he was making headway with her death. Chase handed over the bills and threw the change into a fundraiser bucket. He picked up the grocery bag, but hesitated.

"A mile or two back I saw a woman walking alone. She was soaking wet, dressed in a long white gown.

Should I call someone to look for her?"

"Whaaaaaaat?" The clerk's mouth fell open. "You saw Hannah G.? Where?"

"Just past the carnival. Should I call the police? She might need help."

"No, but you can call Ghostbusters," the cashier said and then laughed at his own joke. "Hannah's dead."

"What do you mean?"

"I'm saying you saw a ghost. Hannah jumped from the pier back in the nineties. Man, you must be something special. No one's seen her walking that road for years."

"No, no, this person was real. I swear." The last word trailed off. Chase squeezed his eyes shut trying to bring back her image. He would have sworn she was flesh and blood, but now he wasn't so sure. Was it his headlights or did she have an aura around her?

Evergreen Drive narrowed as it approached the lake. The earthy scent of summer drifted in through the car's open window as sand and pine needles got caught up in the SUV's tires. The road dead-ended at a pair of slender trunked willows standing guard at the entrance swaying in the evening breeze. The beautiful willows left a lump in Chase's throat.

A cedar-shingled home with a wraparound porch and cadet-blue shutters was framed against a starlit sky. A white plaque with the name Will-o'-the-Wisp and the year 1904 was emblazoned in gold and mounted on a detached garage. Every inch screamed Peyton.

Chase grabbed the groceries and lumbered to the front door. Learning how to uncouple and live just for himself had turned into more of a challenge than he cared to admit. Without her, his step had slowed as a hollow sense of loneliness crushed his chest.

Chase stepped across the threshold. Minus a bride. He hit the light switch, flooding the room in a warm glow. Fawn colored rugs covered wide planked floors that ran the length of the living room into a state-of-the-art kitchen. Peyton had left the stone fireplace and timbered ceiling intact and furnished the space with dark oversized furniture, giving the home a rustic-modern feel.

The smell of leather and hardwoods drew Chase further into the room. He set the groceries on the counter and explored the rest of the house. Down the hallway were two bedrooms and two matching baths. He dropped his duffel and headed toward the opposite end. A hall bath and laundry room butterflied each other. One door remained closed. Chase reached for the glass knob and turned. It wouldn't budge.

"That's odd."

He rattled the knob while pushing his shoulder into the door. The solid wood creaked with the effort but remained stuck. He decided to leave it until tomorrow and put his bags in the bedroom. A large painting of a red lighthouse hung above the bed. Heavy gray clouds surrounded the tower while a violent seawall of white-capped waves crashed into the foundation.

Chase liked the darkness of the painting. It matched his present mood.

The next day Chase stepped out onto the porch with his morning coffee. He cradled Peyton's favorite willow tree mug. It was his first daylight glimpse of the outdoors. Four white Adirondack chairs sat evenly spaced on the wooden porch, painted the same cadet blue as the shutters. A lake breeze gently rocked a swing back and forth.

A patch of green lawn gave way to wild summer grasses and tall cattails, their brown cobs reaching for the sun. Just beyond the dunes, a blue lake absorbed the reflection of the clouds as a lacy wash of waves rushed onto the sand.

The sound of laughter drifted toward him as he walked barefoot down to the water's edge. A little girl ran along the beach, totally engaged in chasing seagulls. A woman trailed after her. She wore a flowing white dress with puffy sleeves. Sunlight filtered strangely through their bodies.

"Hey," Chase uttered, barely able to get the one word out. It looked like the same lady as the night before, except this time she wasn't wet. Her golden-brown hair blew off her neck in waves. She turned toward him and Chase could see an amber light that shone from within. And then they were gone.

"What the...?" Chase fell back onto the sand, unable to breathe. This had to be the most incredible thing that had ever happened in his thirty-two years. He just saw a ghost! That's what the clerk had called her. But nothing about her was scary; in fact, in the bright sunlight she seemed peaceful.

"Yoo-hoo, excuse me, I'm looking for the owner of the house."

Chase shielded his eyes. On the top of the dune stood a woman with reddish hair and skin splotched with freckles. Slung across her arm was a yellow insulated bag with the words Grand Haven Public Library.

"You found him." Chase got to his feet and brushed the sand from his shorts. He took a deep breath to steady his racing pulse and glanced down the beach.

"Do you mind terribly if we head back to your porch? The sun will turn me into a lobster."

Chase pressed his lips together and glanced at his watch. "I guess I have a minute." But really, he wished the woman would go away.

"I'm Patricia Davis. Here, this is for you." She handed him the thermal lunch bag. "It's filled with coupons and gift cards from our local businesses."

"Thanks. I'm Chase Andrews. Good to meet you." He forced himself to be polite and concentrated on giving her his full attention, but every time he heard the raucous squawk of a seagull his interest was pulled back to the beach. Chase led her to a shaded corner of the porch.

"Well, welcome to the neighborhood," she said with an awkward laugh, taking a seat in one of the Adirondack chairs.

"How can I help you?" Chase tried to keep the sharpness from his tone. He wasn't in the mood for visitors and he had work to do.

"My visit is twofold. I'm the library archivist. And I'm here to document your sighting last night. We take our ghost encounters very seriously."

"How'd you hear about that?"

"You met my son, Kyle. He works at the Quik Stop. Did he happen to tell you the details surrounding Hannah's death?"

"No."

"Hannah's story has developed into somewhat of a legend. There are those who suspect foul play, but relatives closest to her weren't surprised that Hannah fell from the pier. She was such a clumsy child growing up. Always in and out of the emergency room."

"Your son said she jumped."

"It's one theory, I suppose. But since she was pregnant with her second child, I doubt it. I was wondering if you noticed the color of her eyes? Hannah was born with brown, yet people who have gotten close enough say they shimmer a deep watery blue. Did you notice that?"

Chase hesitated and thought before he spoke. "I didn't notice the color of her eyes. Like I told your son, she was barefoot, dressed in white, dripping wet." Chase clamped his mouth shut. For now, he wanted to keep the second sighting to himself. It wasn't anyone else's business.

"Hannah grew up in this house. After she married, she and her husband decided to move clear across the state. They were very young. I believe Vincent had just graduated from college."

"Hannah grew up in *this* house?" Things were getting stranger by the minute, considering he hadn't even been in this little Michigan town for a full twenty-four hours.

Patricia Davis nodded.

"You mentioned foul play? What's that about?"

"Vincent was definitely a suspect. Husbands usually are in cases like that. But a neighbor claimed Vincent's car never left their home in Grosse Pointe, and that she spotted him outside with his daughter around noon."

"Sounds like a pretty tight alibi."

"It was. But some folks still think he may have been involved."

"Why? Was he known to be abusive?"

"No, nothing like that, but Vincent ran with a tough crowd. Most of the guys were from the high school football team."

Chase snorted and bit back a sarcastic reply. He rubbed his shoulder where an old injury still plagued him from his days as a running back. "Hey, I got a conference call I need to set up," he lied. "Can we pick this up another time?" He hated being rude, but he remembered the room that he couldn't get into the night before, and now he wanted to find out what was behind that door.

"One last thing," Patricia said as she descended the steps. "Witnesses claim Hannah asks to be taken to her parent's cottage. Did she speak to you?"

"No, she didn't."

"Well, here's my card if any other details come to you."

Chase waited for her to leave before he headed to the garage to look for a screwdriver. The smell of mold and gasoline hung in the air as he swung open the old wood door.

Damn, Peyton, what a mess. Piled high from floor to ceiling was every stick of out-of-date furniture from the cottage. Chase climbed over a mountain of rolled up carpets and made his way to the rear of the garage to the tool bench. He rooted through the drawers until he found a screwdriver and then retraced his steps through the maze of furniture. Scaling the carpets, he lost his footing and stumbled into a wall of beach chairs that hung from a row of rusty pegs. One of the folding chairs came crashing down on his head.

"Shit!" He rubbed the side of his face where a jagged edge had scratched his cheek. A dusty portfolio swung from the same hook that held the chairs. It seemed out of place. Chase pulled it down and unzipped it a quarter of the way. Paintings were inside. He carried the brown leather case back to the house along with the screwdriver.

Outside the jammed door, he loosened the pins on all three hinges, clutched the doorknob with one hand and one of the hinges with the other and lifted. As the door came loose, he stumbled back with it, and set it against the wall.

His first peek into the room revealed a dark paneled bedroom. Peyton's words echoed in his head. *There's a room perfect for a man cave. I've left it as is, so that we can finish it exactly how you want.*

Dust spiraled in the light that filtered through faded curtains. A cream-colored iron bed faced the window with a neatly folded pink quilt at the bottom. The narrow closet remained empty but held the faintest scent of cedar. The rest of the room smelled dank, musty, as if the lake had somehow permeated through the walls. In a corner, a blank canvas rested on a wooden easel, along with a paint box, palettes, and dried tubes of paint. A set of brushes rested on a scrap of linen.

The entire room was caked in a dusty layer of grime. Chase ran his fingers along the windowsill, trailing a path through the grit. He brushed aside the sheer fabric that fell across the window. The lighthouse was in direct view. At his feet red paint splatters stained the floor. Now, the portfolio made sense. He took it from the hallway and laid it across the bed, opening it full. Elastic straps held paintings of the lighthouse similar to the one that hung over the bed he slept in last night. Some painted against a cloudless blue sky, others glowed against a pitch-black moonless night. There were at least a dozen. All moody, meticulously done, and painted with great detail.

At the bottom of each one, the name Hannah was swirled together with a scripted G. Chase was no critic, but the artwork appeared valuable, painted with an expert hand.

Chase took a good look around the bedroom. He could envision what the cottage might have looked like before her facelift. "What happened to you, Hannah?"

Chase neatly assembled the paintings back into order and secured them into place. His fingers brushed along a heavier grade of paper. He pulled a large brown manila envelope out. Inside were old x-rays with Hannah's name, the date and type of injury listed. The black films showed a wide range of fractures in order of occurrence: her left wrist, fractures to the ribs, a broken tibia, and finally the pelvis. Other x-rays showed trauma to the chest and skull. Chase did the math. Hannah's injuries began when she was three years old and continued into her teens.

Patricia Davis' words echoed in his head. *In and out of the emergency room.* Was Hannah a clumsy child as the librarian had suggested? Or did the angry congressman have a habit of beating up on little girls as well as screaming at his wife?

Chase kept seeing her. He would wake and step out onto the porch and Hannah would be standing on the lawn. Faint rays of sunlight outlined her shape making her look as if she were painted in watercolor. Other times she emerged from the sapphire-blue lake soaking wet, the sun glimmering off the waves. At dusk he would find her gliding down the beach bathed in the setting sun. Living in the house where Hannah grew up and seeing her every day made him feel like he knew her.

The days blended into each other and Chase settled into his new surroundings. He committed his mornings to working with a handful of businesses and organizations that he consulted for remotely. Beside his desk hung the canvas of the willow tree that Peyton had painted. Both Hannah and Peyton's deaths were pointless and awakened a hollow feeling in the pit of his gut, a sensation of helplessness. Peyton had appeared more winded the weeks before she died. Chase had ignored the red flag, only suggesting to Peyton that she shorten her runs. Had he insisted that she get checked out by a doctor things would be so different. Maybe Hannah was like him, trapped in the past. Was there something stopping Hannah from moving on?

At night he'd walk into town to grab a bite and a beer. A few times he'd even run into Kyle from the Quik Stop. Chase was ten years older but still liked to shoot pool with him. Chase would pick his brain about the people of Grand Haven, especially the congressman. Turned out that Hannah's father-in-law, Mr. Reese, still lived steps away from the lighthouse. The weathered bungalow with the squared hip roof was visible from Chase's porch.

Nights were tough. Sleep eluded him. He would eventually find himself drawn to Hannah's bedroom. He convinced himself that he'd be able to turn his brain off if he carved out some time to figure out what had happened to her. He started with the doctor whose name had been written on the front of the x-ray folders. That resulted in a dead end. HIPAA prevented hospitals from sharing any information, even for people long dead. A few days later, he received the lead he was hoping for.

Chase was polishing the chrome on the speedboat when his phone vibrated in his pocket. *Talk to Hannah's father-in-law.* The text message came from an unknown number. Chase suspected it originated from the older nurse he'd spoken with about Hannah. This was the motivation he'd been looking for.

Chase set the wax aside and walked down the beach to the Reeses' bungalow. The front door was open with a mesh screen separating him from a hefty man. He sat in a recliner in wrinkled khakis and a golf shirt, thumbing through a Sports Illustrated. Chase knocked, catching the older man's attention as he looked up from his magazine.

"Hi, I'm Chase Andrews. Are you Mr. Reese?"

He nodded that he was, while returning the La-Z-Boy into an upright position. "You that boy that moved into Evelyn and Walter's place?"

"Yes, sir."

"I've seen you working on that boat of yours. She's got nice lines. What can I do for you?"

"I found a portfolio filled with your daughter-in-law's paintings. I was wondering if you knew where I could send them."

"C'mon in then."

Chase stepped inside. Sunlight poured through the windows, illuminating the mirrored trophy cases that lined the living room walls.

"That's a heck of a career." Chase let out a low

whistle as he checked out the shelves that held countless awards, newspaper clippings and championship day footballs. "I used to play myself. Got a full ride to Michigan State."

"Is that so? My son, Vincent, was a Wolverine," he replied proudly. "Can I get you a cold one?"

"A beer sounds great."

"Whereabouts did you say you're from?" Mr. Reese called from the kitchen.

"Grand Rapids."

"Did you buy the place as a vacation home?"

"No, sir. I'm living here full-time."

"Son, you married?"

"I was." Chase hated labeling himself with the title. "I'm a…widower."

"Same," Mr. Reese replied, handing Chase a beer. "Have a seat. I lost my wife in '85. Cancer got her."

Chase bit back the normal platitudes, deferring to nod in respect. "Hardest thing I've ever had to live through."

"I never thought I'd say this, but I miss my wife's chatter. That woman could talk from morning to night."

"I have a voicemail saved on my phone. I listen to it from time to time just to hear Peyton's voice. Probably doing me more harm than good. But I can't bring myself to delete it."

"You do what you have to do to survive," Mr. Reese said, giving Chase a pat on the back. "My son Vincent is gone too. Same cancer got him." The old man's blue eyes watered as he took a huge mouthful of his beer.

"Really? Sorry to hear that."

Chase cleared his throat.

"So, about those paintings I found, there's also a bedroom in the house that's been kept like a shrine. Hannah's paints and easel still stand in the corner. Since then, I haven't been able to get her off my mind." Chase softened his tone, trying his best not to sound like a reporter on the hunt for his next scoop. "Would you mind if I asked you some questions about Hannah?"

Mr. Reese seemed to appreciate the change of focus as he leaned back in his chair. He smiled. "I nicknamed her 'Giggles' because she was always so serious."

"Did you know her well?"

"Hell, yeah, she practically lived here all through high school. She preferred to hide out in our little shack then go home to her parent's fancy cottage. Something wasn't right over there."

"How so?"

"It was all too perfect. The congressman had his big important job in D.C. Hannah's mother had a hand in organizing most of the charity events in the state. Let's just say they liked to be seen, but not to be seen as parents to a beautiful daughter who needed them."

"Can you tell me anything about the congressman?"

"Walter was born to be a politician. He was out of town most of the time, but when he returned he used to stop here and check on Hannah. He'd make sure I wasn't leaving Vince and her alone. Clearly, it was his parenting skills that needed sharpening, not mine."

"I heard he had a temper."

Mr. Reese shrugged. "Some hush hush gossip about him shrieking at his wife in some private club." He shrugged again. "Probably happened. You can't be that plastic in public and not crack every once in a while."

Chase leaned forward in his chair, eager to hear more. The old man seemed to be in a talkative mood.

"What about her mother?"

"She was too busy being the center of attention. She had an attraction for wealthy characters: mobsters and partiers, but especially night owls with old money who could write endless checks for her fundraisers and Walter's campaigns."

"And Hannah, how'd she fit in with all that?"

"She didn't. Like I said, she was here mostly, helping with dinner and waiting for Vince to get home from practice. If she wasn't at her parents' painting, she'd walk the beach collecting sea glass."

"Oh, which brings me back to the portfolio." Chase said. "I don't feel right keeping it."

"I'll talk to my granddaughter. I'm sure she'd love to see her mother's work. Hannah made a killing peddling her paintings. The Looky-loos and the Fudgies loved her lighthouses. She'd set up right on the boardwalk. I've got one of my own. I'll show you."

Chase followed Mr. Reese into the dining room. A large canvas of a red lighthouse painted against a moody-blue sky hung next to a china cabinet. Hannah had captured the fury of the lake as hostile waves surged into the rocky foundation.

"Was there a police investigation after Hannah died?"

Mr. Reese stiffened. "Why do you ask?"

"I've heard some rumors."

"It got pretty ugly." Mr. Reese said, scrubbing a hand across his mouth as he wrestled with what he was willing to say. "Someone started a rumor that Hannah and Vincent had separated. They hadn't, and I'll tell you this much, Vince would never hurt Hannah."

"So—I take it you'd have seen if they were having problems?"

"I think so. Once a month I'd make the trip to Grosse Pointe and spend a long weekend. I never missed a Grandparents Day or Halloween parade. My granddaughter is my heart. She's twenty-eight now and a fancy lawyer. Followed in her father's footsteps."

He walked over to the fireplace and lifted a portrait off the mantle and handed it to Chase. A pretty young woman with smiling amber eyes stood in a cap and gown holding an enormous diploma.

Mr. Reese took the picture frame from Chase's hands and shuffled to the screen door. Chase took the hint.

"Any idea what happened that day on the pier?" Chase figured he'd push his luck as he was ushered out the door.

"Son, are you sure you don't have a horse in this race? You're asking a lot of questions."

Chase wanted to come clean and tell the old man about his lady in white, but he didn't want to start more trouble. "I guess I've become a little preoccupied with her story," he shrugged apologetically.

"The town likes to talk. But don't listen to their gossip. I saw Hannah that day. She stopped here first. Told me she came back to pick up the rest of her things. She was pretty excited. An important gallery had just sold one of her lighthouses for over three grand and was interested in exhibiting her entire collection."

"So, you don't think she jumped?" Chase asked.

"Hell, no. She was the happiest I'd ever seen her. She was expecting again. I remember thinking to myself that there was truth in the saying that pregnant women had a glow about them. I can still picture her walking off wearing a pretty white dress."

"That's the last you saw of her?"

Mr. Reese nodded. "An hour later, the Coast Guard was all over the lake."

The day dawned with sprinkles then switched to rain as Chase arrived at the Grand Haven Public Library. He searched out Patricia Davis and wrangled her help in unearthing some articles about the congressman. He couldn't shake the idea that Hannah's father could get handsy—typical bully politician.

"Can you give me a time frame?" Patricia asked.

"I'd like to start with the seventies and eighties."

Patricia's bifocals slid down her nose as she peered at Chase from above the rims. "That's quite a bit of material. Anything that old will be on microfiche." She set Chase up in front of the machine, showed him how it worked and left him to his research. He scrolled through the film, stopping when he'd come across an image of the young congressman and his beautiful wife.

Countless pages covered the Democratic National Convention on July 14, 1976, at Madison Square Garden. Walter's photo jumped from the page. He stood proudly shaking hands with Jimmy Carter. Former First Lady Jackie Kennedy Onassis looked on, applauding from her seat in the front row. Chase studied the picture, amused at the oversized lapels on Walter's vested suit. Something about it made him hesitate.

Chase struggled to make sense of what he was seeing. Yes, the guy looked like a jerk, but what else? He stared, practically absorbing the picture. Finally, the date at the bottom of the page, July 14, struck a chord. He'd taken note of that particular day just recently, but where?

Chase laid his head down on the desk to think.

"Looks like you could use a break."

Chase popped up and leaned back in his chair. Patricia Davis stood before him juggling a stack of books and a large brown manila envelope.

"That's it!" Chase said.

Large brown envelope. The date was on the x-ray folder. "Thank you," he said, jumping from his seat leaving the startled woman staring after him.

Chase raced out the door of the library, dodging puddles, and jumped into his SUV. When he arrived home, he headed straight for the portfolio and removed the manila folders holding the x-rays. The congressman was out of town when Hannah's ribs were broken. Well damn.

This information fueled the fire that had already started to intensify inside of him. It was the same all-consuming feeling that had driven him to document every silent symptom he'd missed of Peyton's heart condition.

Chase headed to the Ottawa County Courthouse and requested the police report.

"This is going to take some time," the bored clerk behind the plexiglass window said. "Come back later."

Chase hung outside for a bit, thinking. The Coast Guard station wasn't far. He could see the American flag blowing in the wind. Mr. Reese said they were all over the lake that day. He'd stop there after he got the report.

Close to the second hour, the clerk handed the report over. He took it straight to his vehicle and opened the disappointingly thin folder. Date, time, and location where the body was found were all posted. But not much else. Hannah Reese's death was listed as a water-related accident.

A coroner's report stated that the victim's husband had identified her body. A photo of a partially unzipped body bag resting on the sandy beach showed a glimpse of a white dress. Hannah's skin was rubbed raw in places and her color had already taken on a bluish hue. A stab of nausea bit the back of Chase's throat and he quickly turned to the next page.

The report ended with a few notes written by the detective who was assigned to the case. Most of them covered the whereabouts of Vincent Reese on the day of the accident. A neighbor corroborated Vincent's story that he was home in Grosse Pointe with his five-year-old daughter.

Chase drove to the Coast Guard station, an impressive two-story, brick building.

A uniformed representative greeted him with a smile and held out his hand, welcoming Chase with a good firm shake. "How can I be of help?" he asked.

Chase recounted his interest in learning the details of Hannah's death.

"Are you the one who saw her ghost walking by the lake?"

Chase smiled. "That would be me."

"I've never come across her spirit myself, but it's not from lack of trying. I've driven on Lake Shore Drive too many times to count. Shame what happened to her."

"Did you know her?" Chase asked.

"We're a small community. So I knew of her."

"Was the Coast Guard called? Did they investigate? They're barely mentioned in the police report."

The older gentleman took a moment to answer. "Son, why don't you meet me for a beer after my shift. Best to have this conversation elsewhere. Meet me at Rusty's at eighteen hundred."

Chase got a bite to eat, read the stingy report again and waited until around 5:30 to head to Norton Shores.

Rusty's was a ramshackle old place that sat on the edge of the lake. Chase liked the feel of it even before he stepped through the entrance. The stale odor of spilled beer and the laid-back sound of classic rock surrounded him as he pulled up a bar stool next to his Coast Guard informant.

"I didn't catch your name earlier," Chase said.

"Jack Emerson."

"Chase Andrews, good to meet you, Jack." Chase motioned for two beers to a tattooed bartender who was cleaning up the other end of the bar.

"So, what kind of information are you looking for?"

"What happened to Hannah? Was it really an accident?"

"I was a medic at the time and part of the dive team that answered the call to recover the body. We followed the current and found her pretty quick. She was tangled in an old fishing net floating under a nearby dock. Not sure if it was an accident. Water-related incidents often cover up foul play."

Jack checked the time on his watch before he picked up the story. "She was in bad shape. Her face, nose, and forehead were really banged up. My guess is her head hit the cement pilings when she fell."

"Who called the Coast Guard in? Is that normal protocol?"

"Yes and no. The Coast Guard only becomes involved in maritime matters when there's a belief that a crime has been committed on the water."

"I see." Chase frowned. "Did the Coast Guard suspect foul play?"

"We investigated but no criminal probe was ever launched."

"Why was that?"

"Once the focus shifted off her husband, we were removed from the case and the sheriff took over. We were all a bit surprised when he shut down the investigation and declared it an accidental drowning."

"Sounds like you think there was more to it."

Jack snorted. "It could have been a tragic accident. It certainly looked that way. But I thought it should have been more sufficiently investigated. Hannah grew up on the lake, most likely she was a good swimmer. You never know when you're looking at a premeditated homicide."

Jack cracked open a peanut and tossed the shell to the already littered bar floor. "The whole process was muddled. The pathology report claimed inconclusive evidence to water aspiration in the victim's lungs. Witnesses were never interviewed. Quite frankly, that's two red flags for me."

"Anything else stick out for you at the scene?"

"The EMS vehicles drew a mass of attention to the beach. The police had their hands full keeping the crowds from breaking through the barrier. Folks just wanted to get by to comfort John Reese, his son Vincent and his granddaughter who stood huddled on the other side of the yellow tape. I thought it was odd that the congressman and his wife remained by their black sedan in the beach parking area with their driver. Out of the three, the driver seemed the worse for wear."

A week later, Chase paused in the middle of scrolling through a work email when he heard the sound of footsteps climbing the stairs to his porch. He recognized Mr. Reese's granddaughter from her portrait. She stood on the deck, sandals in hand, as if she'd just walked the beach. She smiled, in a subtle manner, her eyes crinkling when he opened the door.

Chase cleared his throat and uttered a hello.

A flash of light shimmered. They weren't alone. Steps away on the green grass, Hannah stood, glowing brightly against a clear blue sky. Her long white dress fluttered in the breeze.

"Hi, I'm Willow."

"Willow," Chase stuttered, pulling his gaze back to the young woman, "like the tree?"

"Uh, yeah." She shrugged. "My granddad said you found some paintings that belonged to my mother."

"Right, come on in." Chase stepped aside to let her enter.

Willow hesitated once inside, then inhaled deeply and headed for the center of the room, turning slowly as she surveyed the house. "I was only here once, the day of my mother's funeral. I don't remember much, but it looked very different. The walls were darker and the windows smaller. I like it better now. Do you mind if I take a look around?"

"Sure," Chase motioned for her to walk throughout.

Willow headed back toward the bedrooms.

"There's one bedroom that still has its original furnishings. I'm guessing it was your mom's room."

Willow paused when she passed Chase's bedroom and gazed at the painting over the bed. "They're really quite good. I wish I'd inherited some of my mother's talent. I can barely draw a stick figure."

"Same." Chase smiled.

Willow continued down the narrow hallway. Chase kept his distance. The scent of her shampoo filled the space with the smell of coconut, like a day at the beach. Peyton's hair had smelled amazing too, minty, summery and fresh.

Willow entered her mother's bedroom and sneezed rapidly three times.

"Sorry, I hope you're not allergic to dust."

"I'm not usually," Willow said, catching her breath. "Why did you decide to keep this room as is?" she asked, sneezing again.

"I didn't. My wife," Chase paused. "My wife was working on the renovations on her own before she died." Chase shuffled uncomfortably and looked away, catching Willow's surprised reflection in the mirror above the bureau.

"I'm sorry for your loss. Was she sick? I'm sorry, I shouldn't have asked."

"She had a heart condition that went undetected."

"I'm sorry, geez, I keep saying that." Willow looked at him with the same soft, amber eyes from the picture.

"It's okay." Chase shrugged, and smiled, trying to put Willow at ease.

He wanted to tell her about the x-rays that he'd found hidden in the portfolio and his hunch. But something made him hold back. For the first time he felt like an intruder forcing himself on a private family matter.

"Is it okay if I stop back with a car? I'd like to take my mother's easel and her paints."

"Sure."

"Well, I guess I'll see you later," she said, picking up the portfolio. Their gazes tangled as she passed. Her footsteps barely made a sound across the hardwood floor as she made her way to the door. The cottage felt empty without her.

The sun had just begun to dip below the horizon when Willow returned.

"I found the x-rays," Willow said, voice shaking. "Did you know they were there?"

"I did." Chase sighed heavily. "I didn't want to overstep. Please, come in."

Willow swiped at a tear and followed Chase to the kitchen.

"I could use a drink," Willow said.

"Do you like red?"

She nodded, and Chase opened a bottle of wine and grabbed two glasses.

"Can we sit outside? This house is creeping me out."

"Of course."

"Let me help you," she offered as Chase juggled

the wine bottle and the glasses while trying to open the door. They both took a seat on the steps that led down to the lawn.

"You wanna talk about it?" Chase poured them both a glass.

"I feel like I'm all talked out. I showed my granddad the x-rays. He wasn't surprised. When I came across the x-ray of a fractured pelvis, I just broke down. I've been crying for hours; no one is that klutzy."

Chase remained silent and listened.

"Why didn't my grandmother stop it? Was she blind? What kind of person lets their child be hurt like that?"

"I think…it's more like, why didn't your grandfather stop it."

"What? My grandmother was the abusive parent?"

"I'm not one hundred percent sure, but during one incident when your mother was taken to the emergency room your grandfather was at the Democratic National Convention. So, that one couldn't have been him."

"How do you know this?"

"I did some digging."

"Why?"

After taking a long sip of wine he met her gaze. She looked hurt and he felt guilty for holding out on her.

"You saw her, didn't you?" Willow's tone was neither surprised nor accusing. "I know about the legend. Everyone does."

"Yes, I saw her."

"Does she look lost, scared, confused?"

"No, she looks happy. I saw her here."

"Really?" Willow said. A cool breeze off the lake dried the tears that pooled within her eyes.

"She looks beautiful. Radiant."

The sky darkened. Willow inhaled deeply. Chase followed her gaze. He guessed he wasn't the only one that looked for answers within the stars.

Willow returned the same time the next night. And almost every evening for over a week. Chase looked forward to her visits. Interestingly, he hadn't seen Hannah since Willow first arrived.

"You okay over there?" Chase asked. Willow was more quiet than usual.

"I've been wanting to ask you something." Her body folded into itself. She lowered her head as if weighing what she was about to ask. A lock of hair fell across her cheek and she tucked it behind her ear. She was so close that Chase could count the hint of freckles that were scattered across her nose.

"Shoot," was all he said as he grappled with being this near to her and the feelings it invoked.

"My grandfather Walter, who I barely know, lives in a retirement community. His caregiver calls me every few weeks badgering me to visit. He thinks my grandfather is failing and suggests strongly that I visit soon. The thing is, I don't have a relationship with him. My dad rarely let me see Evelyn and him growing up. It would feel weird going there."

"I get it."

"Would you come with me?" The words rushed from her mouth. "I can't do this alone. I asked granddad to come but he told me to leave well enough alone."

Chase nodded. "When do you want to go?"

The next afternoon they set out for Harbor Shores, a private senior community on Orchard Lake. An oversized fountain and an equally impressive gatehouse greeted them as they drove along the cobbled drive. A security officer dressed in a navy blazer made a copy of their IDs before giving them directions to the congressman's villa.

"Wow, are we still in Michigan?" Chase said. Unkempt meadows rolled straight to the water while tall hedges hid the custard-colored homes that sat nestled behind them. Willow cut the engine in front of a one-story villa with a red Spanish tiled roof. She sat immobile.

"C'mon, you can do this," Chase said, putting his hand over hers. Her fingers held tightly onto his. It was enough to send his heart racing. They entered a small courtyard and followed a stone path that led to an arched wood door with a black metal knocker at its center.

A male caregiver dressed in blue scrubs answered Willow's tentative knock.

"You must be Willow."

Willow nodded, and Chase held out his hand and introduced himself.

"Follow me," the caregiver said, leading them through a maze of rooms. He stopped outside a well-appointed bedroom that opened onto a garden patio. An older man with a full head of silver-gray hair sat in a wheelchair staring at the lake as a sailboat skimmed across the water.

"Walter, your granddaughter is here."

The old man turned his head and smiled. His watery blue eyes focused on Willow as she sat down across from him. Chase remained standing.

"Thank you for coming," Walter began. "I've prayed for the day I would finally see you."

"I came because there are things I need to know about my mother, and I think you have the answers."

"Maybe," he said softly. His expression fell as if he'd hoped she had wanted to see him.

"How she died has never been clearly explained to me."

"It was an accident, a terrible accident." The old man's voice trailed off.

"Were you there on the pier?"

"No, no, but your grandmother was. She was meeting Hannah with her portfolio."

"Why the pier?"

"Hannah refused to come to the house. She was being difficult as usual." Walter's voice escalated in defense.

"Do you blame her?" Willow shot back. "I found the x-rays."

"That wasn't me." Color rose in Walter's cheeks.

"But you knew!" Willow said. "You left my mother at home with a monster. It was your job to protect her. Why didn't you leave Evelyn and file for full custody?"

"I fought with her about it, I did! But…I was afraid of my wife…is the truth of it. And afraid of her powerful friends." Walter's voice wavered, his knuckles turning white as he gripped the arms of his wheelchair.

"How could you do nothing to stop it?" Willow moved to the edge of her seat, leaning into him. "You're just as guilty."

"I live with the shame of not coming forward, but that choice would have ended my career in politics, and my livelihood."

"So, you chose your career over your child! She was only three years old when it began!" Willow was on her feet and out of breath by the time she finished. Hot tears pooled in her eyes, threatening to spill.

"Please, please, don't go." Willow's grandfather begged. His fingers trembled as he reached out a hand.

"Tell me what happened on the pier." Willow sat down. Chase wasn't sure what he saw in her face: contempt, doubt, hurt, maybe all three.

"Hannah wanted all of her paintings. She needed them for a gallery exhibition. But Evelyn wouldn't give them to her unless she promised to let us see you. Hannah refused and tried to wrestle the portfolio from her. She lost her footing and fell through a rotted piece of railing."

"My mother knew how to swim. Why didn't anyone try to save her?"

"Our driver who was waiting in the parking lot saw Hannah fall and ran straight for the lake. But the current had swept her away before he could get to her." Walter's eyes filled with tears.

"How do I even know this is the truth? And why would you let my father be investigated?"

"I didn't mean for that to happen. We were in shock. Evelyn convinced me to stay quiet when we learned the sheriff's focus was on your father and not her."

Silence settled over the room. Chase observed Willow's face reflecting her resentment toward her grandfather. Slowly she rose from her chair, settled her purse strap on her shoulder, turned and left without a word.

Chase tried his best to keep up a steady flow of conversation on the ride back to Grand Haven, but he was running out of neutral topics.

"You okay?"

"Yes, no, it's a lot."

"Agreed."

"And sad that my grandfather thought that his years-too-late confession could wipe away all the hurt he caused."

"Do you feel like a walk on the beach?" Chase asked as Willow pulled into his driveway. He hoped she'd say yes. He wasn't ready to say goodnight.

"I could use some fresh air. My head's ready to explode."

They walked barefoot on the soft sand. Chase steered Willow toward the opposite end of the lake, away from the pier. The sun had set long ago and the only light that pierced the darkened sky came from a slim crescent of the moon.

"Am I supposed to accept that my mother's death was an accident? My grandfather has always been a liar; why would this be any different?"

"Thing is," Chase turned her gently toward him. "Maybe…I can't believe I'm saying this, but I think we all need to make peace with the past, and let the people we've lost move on. Obsessing over them only keeps them with us, unable to continue their journey."

"I don't want that. But I'm not sure how to let her go."

"You're not alone. We could figure it out together." He stared at Willow for a second and then reached for her hand. Willow's fingers wrapped around his and he led her down the beach toward what looked like a bonfire.

A white beam, bright and opaque, cut through the darkness. Hannah's figure appeared within the light growing stronger as Chase and Willow approached. She wore a long pale gown that shimmered and flowed around her. Her hair was braided in a golden crown and her eyes glowed a warm amber brown.

"Do you see her?" Chase asked, tentatively. "By the fire."

"Is that my mother?" Willow clutched Chase's arm.

Chase nodded, remaining silent, afraid that if he spoke the moment might be lost.

Hannah smiled at her daughter. Then slowly she turned and walked toward the lake. The moon disappeared behind a cloud, blanketing them in darkness except for a few stars that glittered like silver sequins.

Later that night Chase sat alone on the porch. The northern wind gusted from the lake, setting the swing in motion. Clouds of light, yellow, green and blue, swirled in the air.

Chase stood and dug his fists deep into his pockets. He sensed Peyton. He breathed in her scent, sweet, minty and fresh. It was the way she'd always smelled when emerging from the shower.

"You're here," Chase said out loud. "I hoped you would come." The colors intensified.

"I will always love you," Peyton whispered. "And I wanted you to know that I'm okay." Her presence drifted around him as the sound of rolling waves hit the sand.

"I want you to be happy again," she said.

The noose around his heart loosened when he heard the sound of approval in her voice, freeing him from his grief. A dazzling light flashed a white silhouette of her. And then her colors dimmed as she faded into the night.

We were traveling on a back road, winding through the woods in Hammonton N.J. Outside the night was pitch black ... complete darkness, so dark we had to use the high beams to see the road ahead. Back then we relied on good old-fashioned "Dad Navigation" in our family. However, Dad was a bit lost in the dark this particular night so it seemed to be a team effort looking out for potential darting deer, while making sure to not miss a turn.

I felt happy. I was eleven years old. It was a warm summer night with my favorite smell of honeysuckle in the air. We had just left a birthday party for my cousin. Anytime we visited with family, it included a stop at "Red Barn" on Route 206 so we could pick up fresh Jersey fruit pies to bring as a gift. We were on our way home and were joking about which one of us may have eaten the most pie and why was it that we didn't take some home with us?

Frank Sinatra was singing on the radio.

Suddenly out of nowhere it appeared! A silhouette of a glowing figure, its arms reaching up towards the black sky. As we grew nearer, we could make out a long, flowy, white gown blowing as if a strong gust of wind had kicked up; however, I didn't recall any wind ... in fact there was no wind. As we got even closer the silhouette grew eerier but more clear. It was a woman! Her skin was as white as her dress and was illuminated by what seemed to be moonlight. But I hadn't noticed any moonlight. I looked up to the black sky and saw no moon that night. As I focused on her again, I could make out long, dark, straight hair draping her shoulders... Was her hair wet? What was happening?

My dad slowed the car as we all were stunned. We felt drawn to stop, but we quickly realized that we could not and should not stop!

When we drove past, we watched her until she was out of sight, and she just remained in the same spot with her arms raised up. Yes, she did look at us but it was then that we realized she was a ghost! It was so eerie we couldn't drive away fast enough.

-Hammonton, N.J., 1981

The Stillness of Time

River Eno

"*Johanna ... your name is Johanna. You hail from Austria. Wake up!*"

She woke abruptly. The stern voice faded, resonating like the church bells of St. Paul's. She felt the sun descend under the horizon ... strangely, like an adversary waiting to assault when her back was turned. The haunting tones of the sunset call-to-prayer traveled with the cool night air through the broken windowpane high above her head. A visceral reminder of something she could not truly remember.

She glanced around the small, dark space. The tapestries draped over half the canopy bed were thick and left the room with a pungent, musty odor like a library shut up too long. Her thoughts skipped from scents to sounds to seeing through the darkness, and the confusion roused her further.

Upon sitting, she swayed. Her entire body depleted. Her mouth, dry and sore. She could not remember the last time food had touched her lips.

The rhythmic vocals of the salat al-maghrib pulled her attention back to the outside. She would feel better there, in the night. The breeze would clear her mind. She would be protected at the water. She did not know how she knew, but she was sure of it.

She settled her thin legs over the side of the mattress resting high upon a cedarwood frame. The resinous odor clung to the damp air. The way it did back then, when her new husband had rented the flat. That memory was sharply vague, like yesterday, only not yesterday.

She looked down at the floor. Her long, dark hair in contrast with the faded mosaic tile. A palette of cold to greet her bare feet unless she found her Russian ballet slippers, a gift from Aidan for agreeing to his proposal. How could she not? He was handsome, with a yearly stipend of five thousand pounds from his father's estate, and he made a generous wage as serjeant-at-law to King George. And he loved her. She loved him too. From the first moment she saw him at the king's ball in Bradenburg.

She was different then, naïve ... foolish. She remembered a great many things from that period, and yet, could not remember her last meal. It was difficult to keep track of a life. Time had a way of drifting by unseen.

A book lay open on the bed, "Der Löwe, die Hexe und der Kleiderschrank: Den Chroniken der Narnia-Saga von CS Lewis." She could not remember reading it.

Her withered hands came into focus. The skin of her fingers was lined, her veins stood out in bluish prominence, the nails rough and dirty. A dull ache crept into her chest, and she made a fist, shielding them from sight. She did not understand. But she knew Johanna was her name.

She was sure of that.

Drifting from the shadowy loft, Johanna made her way down the molded white stairs, covered in colorful tapestry. She lifted her long shift of cotton so not to trip. The soft material aroused the pleasant memory of her wedding night with Aidan, an old reminiscence that stood out most vividly, consuming the more recent and ambiguous. She felt a bit lost underneath the material. As if she were fading away.

She considered the large room at the bottom of the stairs, all the way up to the vaulted ceiling. The white walls brightened the chamber even with the night sky peeking in from the arched window in the corner.

The room was cluttered with old furniture and uneven stacks of books. An intricate wooden folding screen stood in the left corner. She absorbed it all, knowing in a peripheral way it was her home, not from any memories of celebrations, but from a feeling of familiarity.

Two large columns standing on either side of the archway led to a vestibule and a wide entry door. Piles of dusty books crowded the tiled entrance, like guards from past times and places. She had no notion of their contents and did not know where they came from or why all had numbers written on them. The room was a puzzle. Each piece unfamiliar.

A long white dress sat draped over a faded Queen Anne chair. She skimmed it with her fingertips. The cool fabric was silky but also thick, substantial. She picked it up, revealing dried splotches of dark crimson on the golden fabric of the seat. The dress seemingly placed to hide the soil. She touched the stains slowly, carefully. She did not think it was her blood. It did not feel like her blood. It did not smell like her blood.

She jerked back, pushing those nonsensical thoughts from her mind.

She turned away. It could doubtfully be cleaned now, a truth that troubled her sense of domestic pride. Why had she not had it cleaned?

Johanna held the simple dress to her body. From the small cap sleeves to the lowest stitching, it was edged with white lace. Removing her shift, she slid the smooth, white cloth over her head and dropped the bed clothing into the chair and over the stains. The bottom hem of the dress was gray, but not filthy, and she noticed a pair of white ballet slippers sat neatly under the chair, atop a few more stains. They were not Aidan's gift nor were they new. She put them on and moved her feet to assess their comfort.

On the end table by the Queen Anne, a small and simple gold cross lay neatly over a tattered and ancient looking bible. The book seemed frail in a way that had little to do with its physicality, and so she did not touch it. A smaller book lay open, a silver tassel holding place.

"Go to the river. They will take care of you. Keep track of the calendar."

The note vexed Johanna, and the room was full of small paintings and little charms of stone, glass and marble, but no calendar. The trinkets had tags with random numbers, like the books — 236 – 167 – 146.

As she moved into the room, the difference in weight from her shift to the dress was obvious, but not uncomfortable, and she pulled the whispering material around the chair and smoothed her hands down the front.

She noticed something sharply imposing in a back corner, shadowed and indefinable. She took a tentative step closer only to realize it was a large, dark wardrobe with two long doors, and at the bottom, two horizontal drawers. It was so deeply set into the corner it almost seemed it was trying to stay hidden; not wanting to draw attention to itself. And yet it was impressive and mysterious, almost beckoning her to see what secrets it housed.

Johanna took steps toward it … and then she stopped. The energy of the piece felt as though it were looming over her, trying to intimidate her with its height and sudden cacophony of wailing voices. Her chest pressed in on itself until she felt dizzy as she clutched her shaking hands.

She needed to be in the open air. The pressure that filled her head since she had awoken traveled down her face and into her clenching jaw. It crawled down her neck, to her spine and out the tips of her limbs. Leave, it said! Go to the river!

There was no purpose to see inside the wardrobe now. None at all. She backed up and turned away from the towering wood — the screaming faded with her footsteps.

She hurriedly made her way toward the vestibule, seeing a small desk along the wall. The surface was burdened with even more books and many ornaments of glass. But in the middle, a quill pen and blotter rested peacefully on a yellow paper calendar. Numbers were etched at the top corner of each small box, dating from the first of April to the thirtieth of May. In the thick margin at the bottom of the page was written:

"Eat continuously or forget and suffer all over."

Only no boxes were checked. What was the date? Where was she to begin?

Johanna picked up the quill and flipped open the ink pot. She dipped the nib, dabbed the red ink onto the jar's edge and put an x on April first. She rolled the blotter over the letter. Out of habit, she thought, more than necessity ... although it was hard to say for sure. Her mind was beginning to feel picked at by invisible fingers. Pieces lying everywhere yet none fit together.

"Eat continuously."

Yes. Eat. She reached into the corner and grabbed a white chador draped over the wooden clothes tree. It matched the dress perfectly with the same lace traveling the edge. She put the cloth over her head and gathered it to her chest as she walked to the entry door. The dingy hem of the dress snagged on the crevices where the paste had worn away, creating a low rasping sound as she moved toward the door. She listened before cracking open the small peep window to be sure no one was shuffling about the alleyway.

The neighbor's large door was identical with the same iron-covered peep window, standing dark and powerful against the whitewashed walls. Johanna saw a newspaper on the ground in front of the door, then glanced about to see if she was alone before closing the window. She laid her ear to the thick wood, again, just to be sure.

Her thoughts jumped over each other. She did not want to be seen or to be amongst people, but she needed to be out of this room and into the night. She needed the river.

Johanna opened the door, nearly kicking over half a dozen packages wrapped in brown paper tied with twine. They were all labeled and numbered as the others — 146 – 160 – 130. She quickly stuffed the packages inside the door and closed it behind her.

The rain had left a sheen on the ground and the air was heavy with scent. She glanced up and down the alley-like walkway, pulling the chador even tighter under her chin. She reached for the newspaper out of habit, like blotting the ink. The language was French. Johanna remembered from her days at court.

Large words framed a black and white picture of a man identified as King Muhammad V. In the coming days he would be negotiating with France for Moroccan independence. The top edge of the paper read 1953 February 18. Johanna thought of the calendar in her room and dropped the paper where she found it.

Flavored tobaccos clung to the humid air, and she peered up into the darkened sky before starting down the white steps of the alley. A sparse string of overhead lamps lit the walled-in route, and she knew she could not direct someone to the river, but she could smell the water, the wet land, and the fish. She had been there before, and she needed to be there now, near the movement and the chaos.

She made her way along the winding passage. The scents and voices of Tangier floated through the doors. Similar combinations of saffron, fenugreek, fennel and anise, and yet each meal and conversation distinctly its own.

She slowed; two men smoked while standing in an open doorway, with two small children playing in the shallow puddles along the edge of the walkway. Dim yellow lighting came from inside the house, similar to hers. The smoke lingered in the air.

Johanna glanced warily at the men, not wanting to draw attention to herself by rushing in the dark. Women were not supposed to be out at this time. It was not safe. One of the men reached out and Johanna jerked back, flattening herself against the wall. He scowled and grabbed the children, shoving them inside. The men moved their bodies together as if to bar entrance from the dwelling. They glared at her. Her fingers tightened under the silk chador. She swallowed painfully and slid herself along the wall and away from them. She remembered those expressions. The anger, the fear. She turned onto an unlit alley as soon as she was able, a touch wider and clear of prying eyes. In this darkness no one wandered. Each door was closed tight to stranger interference.

Johanna hurried down the dusty steps toward the square. Tourists strolled as men finished up the closing of shops and cafes and smoked on designated corners, as was their prerogative. The metal benches in the middle of the square were crowded with people laughing. Conversing in a language she knew well though it was not her own. She kept close to the shops to avoid any unnecessary contact. But the wide-eyed stares and loud whispering commentary of her clothing forced her to move swiftly, and she departed the square on the other side. Shops slowly turned into houses and she pushed past the dwellings. The scent of clear, rushing water hung heavy in the air. She continued toward it.

The street widened. The pavement crumbled and gave way to dirt. Johanna stopped to contemplate the adjustment. It fascinated her, how the town gave way to nature. Yielding to its strength.

A tingling marched up Johanna's back, and she looked up. A man wearing a dark hat and coat stood opposite her, across the deserted street, under a lamp light on a portion of pavement still intact. He stood beside a sign designating the area for the stopping of vehicles. He was older. A waft of smoke drifted toward the sky, and he crushed his cigarette under his shoe.

"Sayidat biallawn al'abyad," he whispered, though it seemed he was close to her ear. Would everyone call her that?

He swallowed and wiped a hand down his mouth and beard.

"Tu ne devrais pas être ici," he said softly, in French, as if telling her she should not be here would make it so. "You are given expensive things," he pleaded in English, seeming to try to find a language she understood. He pointed down the road. "Beautiful gifts from the marketplace to keep you at the river where you belong. Go!" He demanded.

Johanna stared.

He took a sideways step. Johanna mirrored it. Her feet, snug in her damp slippers, ready to move. Her hand tightened on the fistful of cloth she held to her chest. A soft breeze blew the ghostly material against her body, lifting it slightly from her shoulders.

The man turned, painstakingly slow, keeping his eyes on her, as though retreating from a rapacious animal, and he continued to walk slowly, deliberately toward the upper end, toward the marketplace.

Johanna turned with him, her eyes fixed and narrowed. Everything around him grew dark, as if he walked in a spot of light. She heard sleeping animals, insects, the water — and then his quiet footsteps, the acceleration of his heart, his breathing and the small sounds from his throat.

Her foot found the street the moment a brightly painted bus squealed to a halt and purged the man from view. She jerked back and through the vehicle's wide windows, watched him. He found a seat, keeping her in his sight as the transport pulled away.

Johanna looked around the dark area, quiet once

more. A hum of old voices began to echo in her head. She squashed them down; she did not like how they made her feel. Those distant sounds added to her confusion, and now she felt watched. She lowered her gaze to the ground, continuing on toward the river. Her chador flowed behind her.

The streetlamps decreased along with the homes. The woods surrounding the river became dense, and the area filled in with trees and shrubs. In the darkness Johanna's shoulders eased. She loosened her grip on the chador and walked the edge of the long road as it curved down alongside the water. She stopped and closed her eyes to hear the symphony of Mother Nature. As before, the insects walked and burrowed into the earth, wings clicked, legs scratched. The shallow breath of the birds vibrated in their nests. Water rushed over rocks. The leaves slid against one another ... and faint voices echoed.

Her eyes flew open. No! Their conversation was not something she wanted to hear. They were spirits long past, scratching to be let in, but she refused! Rehashing old wounds was pointless. She did not have to relive them to know they were painful.

She wiped the dark tears off her cheeks, staining the chador. She found herself pacing the road. Back and forth she traversed the long curve, her purpose unsure, aggravation growing inside of her.

Where had Aidan gone? What was she supposed

to do here? Who would take care of her, like the book said?

A vehicle hummed down the road. Slowly at first, headlights trailing along the trees, illuminating her for a moment before gaining speed to pass her by. She turned and again walked up the dusty lane, not knowing what she was waiting for. Back and forth she traveled.

On her way back down the slope she saw another set of lights. The vehicle slowed and then stopped. She stared at the illumination against the dark, and she wondered.

Is this what she was waiting for?

Gradually, the vehicle moved forward and then suddenly Johanna felt it would not be prudent to engage with the passengers.

"It is you! You're real!" cried the female excitedly, turning to the driver. "The 'lady in white' is real! Pull over. Pull over!"

"I don't think that's such a good idea, Dee. I didn't even want to come here. We were told to stay away from her."

"Only from that young Spanish girl. The locals in the market said she was alone and needed care."

They were British. Johanna frowned and wondered what London was like since she had last been there. She remembered it so vividly. King George's court at Louis' Versailles was the finest, and everyone knew the Constitution of 1791 would fail! Peasants can be so shortsighted. Why did they think they could rule themselves—

"Do you understand me?" The woman asked, breaking into Johanna's thoughts. "Get closer, honey."

The car pulled onto the side of the road, nearer Johanna.

"Do you speak the Queen's? Are you hurt? Oh my, you look absolutely skeletal. And there's something on your face, dear. Dirt or ... something dark. It looks like she's been crying and maybe has an infection in her eyes?"

The driver shrugged. "I don't like this," he said.

"Don't be ridiculous, Christopher. She's clearly traumatized. Obviously, she was left at the altar by some rogue for her to be wandering around in that dirty gown and headscarf."

"They said she's been here for decades!"

"Oh, that's rubbish! She looks maybe twenty-one! She has pale blue eyes and skin as pale as a sheet! She's clearly English. We can't leave her here!"

Johanna stared as the woman retreated from the vehicle and walked tentatively toward her. Johanna's hands began to shake. This woman smelled very good ... a thought that did not quite make sense to her.

"What's your name, child?" Dee put her arms around Johanna's shoulders. "Come with us. We'll get you to a doctor and have you settled right up. All right?"

Johanna lowered her head as the older woman led her to the car.

"You have been crying." The woman tried to see Johanna's face. "Your face is so ... dirty."

She opened the back door and helped Johanna into

the seat. Dee closed the door with a slam and settled back into the front with Christopher.

"Do you have a name?" Dee turned around. "What is your name?" She asked again, overly loud, as if Johanna might have a hearing or comprehension problem.

"A nevem, Johanna."

"Yo-haana," Dee looked wide eyed at Christopher. "She's a kraut!"

"I believe that's Hungarian, Diedre. Although it does sound a bit German-ish. Perhaps she's Austrian."

"Well, either or, she must understand some English; she answered me." Dee turned in her seat again. "We're going to take you to hospital. Do you know where the closest one is?"

Johanna stared.

"Would you look at that? Hold on, Chris. Don't drive yet; I want to clean off whatever is smeared across her cheeks before more of it gets into her eyes, and I don't want to poke her."

Dee dug into her pocketbook and found tissues. She turned onto her knees in her seat for a better angle.

"Come closer, dear. Let me wipe your face. Come now. My, you are skinny."

Johanna mechanically moved forward. Dee reached her arm back.

"Oh my. It's coming right from your eyes." Dee moved the tissues over Johanna's eyes and around her cheeks, then looked at it. "Wait … is that … is that blood?"

Johanna's hand shot up with lightning speed, grabbing hold of the older woman's wrist, digging her uneven nails into her skin and dislocating her shoulder as she yanked her into the back seat.

Johanna sat in the car, breathing heavily. Each intake of breath was like the first ever taken. Her skin vibrated. Dee's skirt had gone nearly over her head, her body crunched in half and stuffed behind the passenger's seat. Christopher's body lay over Johanna's lap. His head and arm on the back of his wife's exposed thigh. There was a gaping hole in the bottom of his throat, messy and leaking all over Johanna's white dress. The pale interior of the car was wet and smeared red. Fighting made it look so very bad. Raw and ugly. Her chest ached at the sight.

She could still hear Dee screaming. She felt Christopher's hands on her shoulders trying to pry her off of his convulsing wife. He had opened the car door, and Johanna had pulled him inside. She had ripped into the part of him that was closest to her teeth. The blood burst into her face before she covered it with her mouth and fed until she could fit no more into her body.

Johanna closed her eyes. Strength roiled through her. She breathed deep, focusing to keep her mind still. She absolutely hated this part. This was why she chose abstinence. Memory loss and confusion were superior to coherency and recollection. She fought to hold her mind in one place.

To no avail.

The voices came, and the memories rushed in like high tide.

2

Aidan held Johanna's hand as they walked along the gangway and off the King George. It was sunny after many days of rain, and the gull's chatter was almost too loud to speak over. Aidan planned their honeymoon to coincide with his solicitor duties to the King. The trip began in France, stopped in Spain and now Tangier. As beautiful as the ocean was, Johanna was quite pleased to be on dry land.

She smiled, feeling her fortune. Although theirs was not a royal marriage, like her cousins Valentin and Larissa on her mother's side, once removed, Aidan did work for the King. He was diligent and trustworthy. And he was experienced, having been to the colonies and back, promising to teach her everything he knew about the world. She was blessed to find a husband so willing to share his education.

He had found a lovely apartment in a quaint section of town, where the streets were narrow, and one could get lost if they did not know their way. It was near the town square where he would work. And like so many buildings in this land the façade was bleached white, the inside ornately furnished with colorful tapestries and tiles. It was close enough to the river that Johanna could walk — escorted, of course. It would not do for her to be alone in a strange land with strange men and even stranger daily customs. Aidan had paid handsomely for her escort of two local handmaidens and two guardsmen.

Aidan left Johanna during the day, to wander the market with her maidens in tow. She thought the people exotic and the food more so. Spices in London were a fortune per ounce, but here, they sat in large sacks or baskets. She had never seen such vivacious and imaginative things. The vibrant fabrics, scarves and dresses. London and France could not boast such beauty and having so much time on her hands to shop, she purchased gifts for her mother, her sisters, her brothers' wives and her cousins, who for all their noble finery, had never been to Tangier.

Aidan accompanied her to dinner every evening, even on the nights he had to go back to his chamber.

"To Johanna…" He stood, always embarrassing her. She giggled when he raised his goblet. "My lovely, one and only, Madonna."

He offered her unique dining experiences, even supping at the houses of colleagues, who were stationed permanently in Tangier, and all too happy to entertain a fellow westerner.

It was at just such a dinner where they met Colonel Konstantin Rathbone. A tall, dark-haired man with pale skin and the iciest blue eyes Johanna had ever seen. She was told he was with the Wallachian army, but he had not disclosed why he was in Tangier, insinuating only that the Ottomans were the cause. Colonel Rathbone spoke briefly of his family, a line that hailed back to Michael the Brave of Wallachia. He turned out to be funny and quite a good listener, and so Johanna invited him for lunch at a restaurant near their flat, to which he politely declined for the reason that he too, like her husband, had to work during the daylight hours.

The weeks passed in a hurry. Aidan still managed to share evening meals with his new bride, though it became more difficult after a colleague returned to England. They had pleasantly run into Colonel Konstantin at three more engagements. Amongst the many guests Johanna did not know, the Colonel was a familiar face, and his easy, dare she say eager, demeanor made her feel welcome and calm. His compliments always gave a sweet flutter to her stomach. She was pleased her appearance had not suffered under the weight of the loneliness that seemed to be gathering around her. It had been so long since she had seen her family.

One evening while shopping late Johanna thought she saw the Colonel across the square. And again, in a darkened alley when Aidan dropped her home before going back to work. She had to be imagining things. The Colonel was too dignified to linger in alleyways. Aidan told her the strain of being away from home could make her see things, and that she should rest more. But she did not want to rest. She wanted to see her family.

One rainy afternoon Johanna received a surprise note from the Colonel asking her to dine with him that very evening. She was in the middle of declining when her husband's porter knocked, telling her Aidan could not take her to supper, and that he had advised Colonel Rathbone to call, if it pleased her.

She was most disappointed, because she knew how Aidan missed her and she missed him. But it did please her to eat with the Colonel. She had such fun with him, and so she returned her reply promptly.

She dressed for dinner on the far side of the large living area with the help of her handmaidens before they retired for the evening. The bedrooms in Tangier were what Aidan called lofts and there was only room for a bed, a small table and her wedding outfit that she had hung by the wall near the stairs. Aiden teased her, but it reminded her of home and made her as happy as the day she wore it each time she saw it. Her French armoire, much too big for the loft, was placed in a discrete corner downstairs. And with the large, beautiful dressing screen Aidan gifted her — voila, a dressing chamber.

Johanna knew she spent too much time deciding what to wear, but it was only because she did not want the Colonel thinking her naïve or ignorant. Her efforts were rewarded when the guardsman guided him into the parlor from the vestibule. His blue eyes widened as he gazed upon her.

"Why, Lady Johanna, you are a vision."

His familial accent was just under the surface, and Johanna found it extremely charming. When he kissed her hand, she blushed and looked down as was polite.

"Aidan is no lord, sir," she gently corrected. "And I am no lady."

"You are to me." Rathbone smiled, his blue eyes

brightening almost frightfully. He held out his arm. "Come, let us eat."

At the small inn, the Colonel had but to ask a question before Johanna opened up. She confided her love of gothic romantics, Shakespeare and the medical journals she secretly stole from her father's library and studied when she was alone. A confidence the Colonel swore to keep.

"I may have said before, I was born and raised in Austria until I was nine. Then I was sent to France for tutoring. My great, great, great granduncle was Herzog Frederick V of Baden. No wait, I apologize. Duke of Baden." She smiled. "Aidan corrects me to use the western aristocracy terms."

"Yes," said Rathbone uneasily. "I remember Herzog Frederick IV."

"Excuse me, sir." Johanna giggled. "You are too young to know my granduncle let alone his father."

"Of course." Rathbone stood corrected. "I meant only that I know of him and his legacy."

"Oh." Johanna nodded. "I see, yes." She took a sip of wine, motioning to the Colonel's full plate of meat, beans and potatoes. "Will you not eat?"

"I beg your pardon."

"Your meal, sir." Johanna motioned to his plate again. "Will you not eat? Are you not hungry?"

"Oh … yes. I am." Rathbone smiled, perhaps awkwardly. "See there, I have eaten. Nearly every bite."

Johanna looked at the Colonel's empty plate aside from a few small potatoes. "Oh my … oh, I … I could have sworn your plate was full." Johanna laughed and set her wine glass back on the table. "Perhaps I have had more to drink than I ought."

Rathbone's smile broadened, and Johanna smiled back.

"Tell me more about your sisters." Rathbone's blue eyes blazed. "Will they visit you here?"

It had been four months to the day since they set foot in Tangier. Johanna was most homesick, although rarely disclosing her feelings to Aidan. A proper wife was supportive of her husband and did not burden him with any weakness of spirit. But she saw so little of him, and so much more of the Colonel, the local people were beginning to think they were married. Not to disparage the Colonel. He was decorous and handsome, promising he enjoyed hearing the boring stories of her family. However, Aidan was her husband, and she did not ever want to appear improprietous or brazen.

Arriving home late one night, after escorting her to the small theatre, the Colonel offered to enter her dark apartment to light the lamps. An unmarried man entering her apartment when no one was home was certainly improprietous. Only, she did hate to stumble about the dark like a clumsy fool.

The Colonel gave Johanna his top hat and cane to hold while he used her key to open the door. However, it was open, and the vestibule was dimly lit from the lamps inside. Upon entering they saw Aidan, sat in the new Queen Anne chair at the bottom of the steps. Waiting.

"Rathbone." Aidan's tone was dark, causing the room to remain still for a moment. The deep smudges under his eyes aged the young man beyond his years. His high collar was pulled open, a small and simple gold cross laid on his bare neck.

Rathbone's expression blackened.

"Why are you sitting here alone, husband?" Johanna hesitated, then seemed to realize where Aidan's attention was focused and embarrassingly took her hand from the Colonel's arm.

"Waiting for you, my wife."

"We were at the theatre. Do you not remember?"

"You did not tell me you would be gone half the night."

"Half the night? Aidan … that is, yes, it is late … but you are usually gone … I have not seen you for two days."

"Does that mean my bride is to be gallivanting all over town whilst I toil?"

"No, Aidan, I …"

Johanna's eyes filled with tears. She felt foolish and turned away from both men.

"Do not be cross," said Rathbone. "This was my doing. I knew the play would end late."

"This is your doing," agreed Aidan, and he walked past the older man to the vestibule. "Please, see your way out."

Rathbone looked at Johanna. He set his jaw and turned to Aidan.

"Goodnight, Colonel," said Aidan. When Rathbone made no move to leave, Aidan raised his arm to show him the door, a small black bible gripped in his hand. "It is late, and I would hate to have to ring the guard at this hour."

When the door lock clicked, Aidan made his way to Johanna. He took her arm and yanked her around.

"How could you do this to me? Make me look like a fool!" He smacked Rathbone's top hat from her hand and grabbed his cane. "Eating with him every single night. Going to shows. Not bothering to come home until such an hour!"

"But you told me to dine with him! You told me to go!"

"Not every night! Could you not see, he is not what he pretends to be! Now I hear stories—"

"What stories? What do you mean? Please Aidan, I am lonely!"

Aidan raised the cane at her impertinence. Johanna's eyes widened in horror. She burst into tears and ran up the stairs to the loft. Aidan's footsteps sounded behind her as he raced up to find Johanna sobbing face down on the bed.

"I am sorry, Johanna," he said after a moment, then slowly sat next to her. "I told you when we first met you had never fear me. Can you ... can you forgive me?"

Johanna sat up, stilled when she saw the cane in his hand. He threw it into the corner, crashing into Johanna's small night table set tightly between the bed and wall. He wiped the tears streaming down her reddened cheeks.

"Forgive me," he whispered. "I am a jealous man, and Rathbone is a liar and a reprobate!"

"Oh, Aidan!" Johanna threw herself into his arms. "I am so sorry."

"No, it is I who am sorry." He pulled back, his expression far away. "This trip has not been what I expected. Listen to me. Pack your things. We will leave in two days' time."

"Oh, Aidan, do you mean it?"

"I do. Let us be gone from this place."

"Thank you, husband! Thank you!" Johanna hugged him and jumped up. She practically raced around the bed to gather ribbons and scarves and shoes she had placed on and around her little table. "I cannot wait to see mother! My sisters… I will have to write first thing in the morning if news of our arrival is to get there before we do. No, I shall do it tonight! Also, our home, it has been shut up for months, who will open it? I could ask—"

A strange sound stopped her considerations. Johanna turned, then startled back into the wall. Her shoes and ribbons dropped to the floor. Colonel Rathbone stood behind Aidan at the top of the stairs.

"What are you doing here?" Johanna asked.

She could not understand the scene that unfolded before her. Aidan was holding his throat, gasping. The Colonel was holding him, keeping him on his feet. Aidan tried to speak, but only gurgles came through. Blood seeped through the fingers at his throat and down onto his shirt.

"He will not take you from me. Not when I have been so fortunate in finding you." Rathbone shoved Aidan forward, letting him fall onto the bed.

"Aidan!"

"No, no!" Rathbone cried as Johanna reached for her husband. "You are my prize! My consolation."

"Please," Johanna sobbed. "What do you speak of?"

"What amazing luck to find you here." Rathbone ruminated, his eyes wild. "My family line always was rather blessed." He grinned at the word.

"I do not understand, sir." Johanna pleaded, staring at Aidan on the bed.

"Of course, you do not understand. You are stupid. Now look at me!" He snapped his fingers to gain her attention. "I was the reason Frederick IV came by his title, Johanna. Promises were made. Promises were not kept." He pointed at her. "On your family's side!"

Johanna shook, desperately wanting to hold her bleeding husband.

"Your great, great, great, great granduncle used me and then locked me up. For decades!" The distain in Rathbone's voice sent Johanna over the edge, and she screamed.

Rathbone dove toward her, putting his hand over her mouth.

"Please," she mumbled under his hand. "Do not hurt me."

"Hurt you? You stupid woman..." Rathbone smiled, his teeth much like the Austrian lynx as it hunts. "I am going to make you, and your sisters, mine ... forever."

3

Johanna returned to herself, to the backseat of the car, as if dropped into her body from above. The couple from London, leaking and dead, tangled around her. She hated this. She hated it all.

She now remembered her husband's last moments, and her insides began to seethe, as they had back then. She shoved the man off her lap, climbed through the car door with a thunk and hit the ground running. Her ballet slippers tight around her feet. The soft shoes noiseless as she raced up the hill, back to her home. Too fast to see anyone. Too fast for anyone to see her. Thinking only of Aidan.

She burst into the vestibule. The door slammed against the wall. She saw the new packages on top of the old books and the trinkets, all numbered. 135 – 146 – 159 – 160. She looked at her door, Apt 147. She turned to see the door across the alley. Apt 146. These were the offerings from the humans, to keep them safe. Sustenance brought the memories, clear as if they had happened yesterday.

She closed the door, realizing her chador was still with the couple she had killed. She did not care. The humans would clean it up for her. As always. She walked through her room with enlightened eyes. She touched the trinkets of stone and marble, and the voices of the men and women echoed in her head.

"Can you understand me, girl?" The tall one had asked in heavily accented English. "You cannot go home, nor see your family again. But we will take care of you... if you can promise to leave us alone, keep us safe from others of his kind, of your kind."

"You can stay here for your days," the small plump woman had said. "Keep us safe, and we will send you food at the river, away from the town folk."

"We will give you all the pretty things a girl could want. We will take care."

They towered over her, pleading, knowing she could tear them to pieces.

"I want books," Johanna whispered as she wept. "All kinds. And dresses, like that one." She pointed to her bloody wedding gown laid over Aidan's body.

They had looked at each other and then nodded to her. She did not know if she would ever understand why they took pity on her. Perhaps she did not appear deadly. But they knew what she had done.

Rathbone came back for her. He found her as she awakened, the sunset prayer tones echoing loudly through the apartment. Her body half covering her dead husband. When she saw him enter the loft, she slid off a pile of white material, scraping her back on the edge of the small table in the corner. Rathbone walked around the bed and stared down at her.

"I do not feel... right," whispered Johanna. "What have you done to me?"

"For the first time in your insipid, meaningless life, you finally are right, my dear. You are quite lucky to have been given a new existence. By all accounts I should have killed you, familial blood for your ancestor's transgression. Never forget, I am the benevolent one here."

She tentatively reached up and touched Aidan's hand hanging motionless off the edge of the bed.

"What have you done to us?"

"What have I done? I merely wounded him, Johanna. You drank from him. Do you remember?"

She cringed. She knew what she had done. He told her it was how she had to survive, threw her wedding dress at her saying she was now a princess of the dark. She used the dress to try and stop Aidan's bleeding. He forced her face to the hole he had made in Aidan's throat.

"You took all his blood. Like a ravenous animal," he said. "Hardly necessary to survive. That was your choice alone."

Johanna felt her blood begin to boil in her veins. An unnatural rage like nothing she had ever felt. Disgust rose into her throat like bile. Her hand clenched the pile of ribbons on the floor, her nails dug into her palms.

"You killed him," he said. "You did that."

Johanna shifted to her knees, hitting Rathbone's cane Aidan had tossed into the corner the night before.

"You are the killer here, Johanna. Not I."

Johanna stood slowly, deliberately, curling her hands around the walking stick, using it to push herself from the floor.

"You are right," she whispered. "I am a killer."

"Yes," Rathbone smiled, opening his arms for his new daughter. "Come to me. Embrace who you are. We will do great things as I guide your monster."

"If I am a monster, sir…" Johanna inched her way

out of the corner, fury moving her feet. Newly gained instinct guiding her step. "I am what you made me."

The rest was always a blur. A literal flurry of actions. Johanna could never remember her thoughts at that moment. She did not think she had any. Only feelings of wrath and revenge and instinct. One moment Rathbone's ice blue eyes were blazing, his fingers digging into her arms, his face burning with conquest and pride. The next, the silver end of his cane came bursting through his mouth, thrust up from the sternum. Johanna pulled the ends of the cane until the entire staff ripped free of his chest, yanking out his lungs and heart and ribcage and covering her in blood.

Johanna had no idea how many days later they came. The local men and women. Quietly. They calmed her. They undressed and cleaned her, then presented her with the compact that has kept her in Tangier to this day.

"Put the dress with him," Johanna instructed weakly as they gathered her wedding gown and Aidan's body. "Keep him close."

4

Johanna turned to the overbearing wardrobe in the corner. She walked to it. Her limbs like lead and yet she was eager to see. She pulled the knobs and opened the large doors. A white wedding gown hung still and silent. A matching chador next to it. Items used only once, then given to her as tribute, as she had asked so long ago. She went to her knees and reaching into the bottom of the wardrobe, she wrapped her hand around a pile of wedding cloth, darkened from aged blood and tattered from time. Moving the decrepit fabric aside she revealed her only love. The only man to ever touch her and know her body the way two people are supposed to. Her husband. Her Aidan. They had done what she asked and kept him close. Still wrapped in the beautiful funeral blankets of the era, now ragged, the white of his skull showing through.

Johanna wept.

She stripped off her bloody gown and laid it in the vestibule. They would take it for her. She went to the opposite corner and cleaned herself in the basin of water that was always filled and tucked behind Aidan's changing screen. She ran her fingers down the carved wood. It showed wear but was still wildly beautiful. Her heart ached for him, for all she had lost, for all she had done since ... for everything.

Johanna reached into the armoire to take down the new gown and place it on the Queen Anne chair. She hesitated. She looked around the room at all the tributes. She was not quite living up to her end of the bargain, keeping them safe. She felt abrupt guilt for that.

She went to the chair and pulled her shift over her head. It fit better now that she was nourished and healthy. The calendar was supposed to help her keep track of her days. It was useless. She always slept too long. She forced herself to. When she was fed and awake her life played like a reel of bittersweet memories, ever rolling, on and on.

And while sleep and abstinence made her forget, atrophied her mind... when she woke, she did horrid things. She was not sure the bliss of disremembering was what she wanted anymore. She pulled the calendar page off the desk and threw it away.

Johanna grabbed one of the new gifts wrapped in paper and took it to the loft. She hopped onto the bed with ease and opened the wrapping. The book was old. The inside said it was a first edition, printed in London in 1764, "The Castle of Ontranto." She knew the story and smiled. The movement felt foreign but welcome.

She read quickly as her preternatural mind allowed until she heard the first tones of the Salat al-fajr. Sunrise was upon her and the call to prayer sang through the broken windowpane. The beauty of it nearly mesmerized her. She lay back, acknowledging over a century and a half of cruelty, and wondered if it would ever change... could it, could she, ever change.

She would sleep now. But she thought she would wake the next night, go to the river and pick her food with care. Feed on the deserving, not the unsuspecting, to keep her town safe. What she was doing, she thought, was not who she was. It certainly was not who Aidan believed her to be. She thought she could maybe stop the cycle if she was strong enough to let go the burdens of guilt and shame.

Perhaps she could finally comprehend that when someone breaks your trust it does not show damage to your character but shines a glowing light on the holes in theirs. She could have done nothing differently to save Aidan. She had been sure of that for a long time.

Unable to keep her eyes open, she remembered Aidan's face and his love. And she caught a glimpse of the strong voice that was always in her head when she woke.

Her voice.

Your name is Johanna. You hailed from Austria. You reside in Tangier. You will uphold your word. You will protect those who protect you.

She was sure of it.

This happened to my friend Gina. A neighbor who lived directly across the street [from Gina's house] claims he saw a lady in a long white gown walking back and forth in front of her house.

Earlier that day, a restraining order had been issued against Gina's sister's boyfriend. Both Gina and her sister believe this spirit patrolled the road in front of their house in order to protect them from harm.

-Turnersville, N.J.

Waitin' Round the Bend

Melissa D. Sullivan

Eleven p.m. to six a.m., no matter what corporate bullshit appeared on Nick Cardoza's paycheck, was the graveyard shift. And the graveyard shift at an old folks home in the Philly suburbs was as close to death as you could get.

With an aggravated click, Nick opened a link promising "12 snappiest guitar tunes from the 1960s."

A distant voice whispered, and Nick startled up. There, behind the comically large computer screen, was a slight and stooped figure in gray. It swayed menacingly toward him.

"Fuck!" Nick squeaked and jumped up from his chair.

His eyes adjusted from the bright light of the computer screen to the dim of the hallway. Mr. Ratzinger, one of the patients, stood before him. In the low glow of the hall lights, he looked even more undead than normal, with his eyes set far back in his bald, Gollum-like skull above his corporate-mandated face mask.

Taking a deep breath, Nick flexed his arms back, pretending he was just stretching out to get back some of his self-respect. After a few moments, his heart slowed. "Mr. R., you freakin' scared me. What are you doing out of your room?"

Mr. Ratzinger didn't say anything but shuffled in place a little.

"Can't sleep?"

The old man twisted his head to one side, which could have been a "no."

Nick stepped out from behind the desk and poked his head into the main hall so he could see the nurse's station forty or so feet away. Nick's desk was parked at the far end of the Memory Care unit, tucked in a hallway so short it was really more of an alcove. It was pretty ridiculous, really. A new requirement from Corporate because one of the residents had managed to push open the massive emergency doors at the end of the hall and fell or something. Now they had to have someone sitting there twenty-four seven. So they called it the secondary guard station and provided a desk, a cheap ass chair and a computer with double screens that showed all the security feeds. It was Nick's job to sit there from eleven to six, watching the grainy video feed and occasionally do rounds to make sure none of the old folks escaped.

Not that many were mobile. Mr. Ratzinger, for all that he looked like a decaying zombie Deadite from *Army of Darkness*, was one of the patients most often moving about. Nick was supposed to take any wandering residents back to their rooms, firmly but gently, but tonight, he was in a rebellious mood. And shouldn't Mr. R. be rewarded for his escape?

Nick craned his neck, trying to get a clear view of the rest of the hall. He didn't see Aunt Carol or any of the other night staff.

"Come on," Nick said, pointing to a cheap plastic chair next to the desk. "Before Nurse Ratched catches us."

Mr. Ratzinger shuffled around the chair and sat down shakily, his ankles thin and veiny below the hem of his ratty flannel robe. Nick pulled his headphones out of the jack of the ancient desktop and checked that the speaker volume wasn't too loud before clicking on the link. A tinny yet snappy syncopated drum rhythm wafted out of the speakers.

"Whaddya think about this one? Would Corporate approve?"

Mr. Ratzinger looked at Nick, his expression not changing.

Nick checked the video title. "Come on, man. Help a dude out. It's 'Hello, Mary Lou' by Ricky Nelson. Supposed to be the hit of 1961."

No answer. Which was completely expected. He had never heard Mr. R. speak, in the whole four weeks he'd been at Oak Glen and even his nodding seemed more like a muscle spasm than a deliberate response.

Nick sighed and turned back to the screen. The song was a little bluesy for him, but he could probably manage the rhythms well enough and the vocals were easy. But it would be so much better with a second guitar and some vocal harmonies. Alex's angry and disappointed face came to mind, and he viciously pushed it away. With COVID, Oak Glen Manor for Senior Residential Living had nixed all nonessential outside visitors. Even the family members of the residents couldn't come in. So even if Alex had been answering his calls or texts or posts, she couldn't come. Nick was stuck playing a solo noon New Year's Eve concert to a bunch of seniors so out of it, they could be on the moon for all they cared.

Nick sighed again, and clicked over to another page, boasting a complete list of snappy hits from 1961. When the page loaded, a tinny ad started shouting at him about a car warranty, and Nick clicked the mute button.

"Goddamn it, Carol," Nick muttered, and then glanced guiltily at Mr. R. He wasn't supposed to curse in front of the patients, even if they were completely deaf or in a coma. And though Carol was a tough old bird, she was the closest thing he and Mom had to family. She'd even gotten him this gig. It wasn't her fault that it sucked ass and was dull as shit. As unlikely as it was that Mr. R. was aware of anything, it would be shitastic if Carol lost her job. Look what happened to Mom.

"Sorry 'bout the cursing, Mr. R.," Nick mumbled.

Mr. R. nodded or at least his chin fell forward a little, which Nick took as a gracious acceptance. Nick clicked on another page.

"To be fair, it's not even Carol's fault. Not really. It's all Corporate's idea, this whole sixties prom concert thing. For morale, they said. Aunt Carol just had to mention that I play guitar." Nick frowned, Alex's angry face appearing before him again. "Used to." Nick clicked again. "Anyway, not like there's going to be a whole lotta dancing, right?"

Mr. Ratzinger tilted his head to the side, like a judgmental bird.

"You're right, man. That's a low blow." Nick scrolled down the page. "But it's money, right? Five hundred bucks bonus. That's a whole month's rent. How could I say no? I couldn't ask Mom again."

Nick went back to the previous page and started up the lyric video again. "So what do you think, Mr. Ratzinger? Will anyone like this one?"

Mr. Ratzinger squinted his eyes, which could have meant anything.

"Pretty cheesy, right?" said Nick. "Okay. How about some Elvis?"

He clicked on another link, "Are you Lonesome Tonight?" He didn't recognize it, but it had a slow strum, which would be easy enough. With enough gel and his longish hair, he could probably manage the pompadour, which would make a good Insta post. Not that he cared who saw it.

Mr. Ratzinger started to jerk in his chair. No, not jerk. Bop, like to the music.

"Okay, then," Nick said, a little amused. "Elvis it is."

The next Elvis number, "Little Sister," had a decent groove and featured some pretty wicked guitar licks. Mr. Ratzinger was practically tapping his arthritic toes by the end. Maybe he could do an all Elvis set.

Nick clicked over to another page. Prom Hits of the 1960s. Well, it was supposed to be prom-ish. He scanned down the list. Chubby Checkers was groovy but hard to pull without a band. He kept scanning. He clicked and stopped, and then clicked and stopped again. It was a lyric video called "Moon River," which sounded familiar. He clicked and the swoony sounds of an orchestra filled the office. A man's smooth tenor started.

Oh, right. He'd heard it before on one of Mom's movies, and with its lush orchestrations and non-threatening lyrics, it was probably exactly what Corporate wanted. But he would be goddamned if he was going to play shitty smarmy stuff. He had already lost too much over the past couple of months. He wouldn't give up what was left of his artistic dignity, too, no matter how badly he needed the money. He paused the song and clicked over to another on the list.

But a hand clutched his before he could jump the page.

Nick looked up. Mr. Ratzinger had one skeletal hand on his wrist and, Jesus Christ, was he crying?

"Mr. Ratzinger, are you feeling okay?"

Mr. Ratzinger shook his head and pushed Nick's wrist, sending the mouse pointer flying over the screen.

Jesus. Maybe this hadn't been a good idea. Nick x'ed out of the browser.

"Mr. Ratzinger, I think I should get you back into bed."

Mr. Ratzinger didn't move but tapped Nick's hand again, his eyes round and red rimmed. Nick moved his hand away nervously.

"It's okay, man. We'll talk later. Now, come on. Back to bed, before Nurse Ratched prescribes shock therapy for us both."

Usually when Nick got home, he cracked a beer open and, if he wasn't too tired, made a microwave pizza before passing out on his futon. But this morning, after stripping off his scrubs and taking a quick shower, he made a bowl of instant oatmeal and started flipping through the list of songs on his phone.

As the sun was just coming in through his one window, not caring what his neighbors thought, he got out his guitar.

It was his first guitar, an old Yamaha bought used from a music store in the city when he was fifteen. It didn't have the same depth as his Taylor, but he wasn't ready for that yet. He hadn't touched his Taylor since February, except to rewet the humidifier, because he could hear Alex's voice in his head each time he opened the case. Alex was the one who got the price down, pointing out to the bearded sales guy that it was the last one in the series. She talked Nick into buying it with all the money he'd made slinging lattes at the Black Metal Coffee that summer. It was a beauty, though, with a hardwood mahogany top and a rosette of tortoise shell around the sound hole. As soon as he picked it up, the neck felt like it was specifically shaped for his hands.

"It'll be part of your soul," Alex had said.

No, he thought, firmly shutting down the memory. The Yamaha would be fine enough for his current purpose. He strummed, feeling the bite of the steel against his fingers. Damn it. His hands hadn't been this soft since ninth grade. He tuned the strings and pulled up a TAB on his phone for one of the Elvis songs. It was rough at first, but by the time the sun was full out, he had gotten up to a decent tempo. On the final time through, he stopped and let the sound waft out through the apartment. He was actually smiling, sort of. If he closed his eyes, he could picture the crowd at the café, Alex sitting across from him, clutching her Gibson and grinning while the applause washed over him. It had been so good.

But, in his usual spectacular fashion, he had fucked it all up.

Nick shook his head hard once, then again. If Alex wouldn't answer his texts, there was nothing he could do except face the fact that this was his pathetic life now. He would just have to survive it, like Ash Williams and his chainsaw hand against a hoard of approaching Deadites, one grisly step at a time.

The next night, before Nick left for his shift, he downloaded a bunch of songs to his phone so he could finalize the concert playlist. After a moment, he grabbed the Yamaha in its hard case. The gig was only three days away, which didn't give him much time to get his chops back. If anyone complained, he would just say Corporate ordered him to play. Just following orders, ma'am.

When he arrived two minutes after the start of his shift, he was relieved to find the nursing station empty. No witnesses, no crime. But when he turned into the alcove, Carol was behind his desk, searching for something. She and the printed lady bugs on her mask gave him a measuring look as he approached.

"Good evening, Nicholas."

Shit. Nick stopped a few feet from the desk.

"Hi, Aunt Carol." He gave a nervous tap on the case over his shoulder. "Do you mind?"

Carol narrowed her eyes a little and shook her head. "I guess not. Just make sure you don't bother the residents." Her eyes softened above her mask. "How's your mom?"

"Better. Thanks." Nick shifted his guitar back on his shoulder and then paused on a thought. Should he ask about Mr. R.? He was supposed to report on any incidents during his shift, such as any residents taking a walk about, but in his rush to get home, he'd let it slip. Carol never let him get away with anything, so chances were no one noticed. Still, what if something happened to Mr. R.? Maybe he could ask in a completely casual way.

"Hey, is Mr. Ratzinger, like, okay?"

Carol put a hand on her hip. "What did you do?"

Fuuuuuck. She knew him too well. "He got out of bed last night. I forgot to write it up."

Carol's eyebrows rose the way they used to when Nick walked too quickly around her swimming pool.

"Nicholas Antonio Cardoza. Not good." She set down her clipboard. "Did he seem disoriented?"

Nick shook his head quickly. "No, not really. He went back to bed when I took him."

"Okay," Carol said. She closed her eyes and ran her thumb over the crease that appeared over her nose whenever she was stressed. "It's awful, really. His wife passed away last week."

"Jesus. I didn't know he was married."

"She's been at the hospital for two months now, so before your time. Dolores had been on a ventilator for a while, just hanging on. But her lung tissue started scarring and she was gone." Carol's eyes crinkled a little, and Nick could picture her soft smile under the mask. "She was a sweet lady. They came to us together a few years back, and Mr. Ratzinger insisted on being placed in the same room, though she was much worse off than him. Really advanced dementia but still as nice as could be to everyone. He used to call her his daisy, because she was as pretty as a flower. She just adored him."

"Does... does he know?"

The crease appeared between Carol's eyes again. "We put a phone up next to him, so he could see her and say goodbye. But he didn't seem to understand." She turned her head away for a second. "Sometimes I don't wonder if that's better. The not knowing." She paused and then laughed a little. "I remember she always wanted to sit next to him, holding his hand, and he'd sing to her."

"Sing?"

"Oh, yes. Mr. Ratzinger was a minor celebrity in his day. A lounge singer in Philly. A crooner, like Sinatra. Very popular. Very handsome, too."

Nick blinked. It was impossible to think of Mr. Ratzinger in his ratty robe, his jowls hanging, as anything close to handsome.

But he was being an ass. Mr. R.'s wife was dead and that sucked, even if he didn't know what was going on.

"When did she...?"

"Last Friday." Carol gave him that look again. "Did he say anything?"

Nick shook his head. "Sorry about the report."

"It's okay. Just don't let it happen again." Carol leaned down and opened the bottom drawer. "Ah-ha!" She pulled out a box of pens, pulled a couple out and stuck them in her pocket. She picked up the clipboard and held it out to him like she was offering a ceremonial shield. "Care to join me? I'll do West if you take East."

Nick nodded quickly, chucking his coat behind the desk and tucking his case in the leg space. Motivated by guilt, he tried to do rounds as perfectly as possible. At each door, he peered in the small glass window, checking to see if the residents were in their beds, putting precise X's as he went. Most of the rooms were dark, save the eerie green lights of the machines. Other rooms flickered with silent TV sets. When the residents were asleep, Nick stepped quietly in and turned the sets off.

At the last room at the end of the East hall, Nick hesitated. Mr. Ratzinger's. The door was slightly open and one lamp was on, but Mr. Ratzinger, too, appeared asleep, his eyes closed, his mask dangling off one ear. The TV was silently showing some scene from a black and white movie. The bed next to him was flat and empty, the white sheets pulled tight as paper. He always thought it was just ready for a new patient. But as he looked around the room, he saw things that had to be Mrs. Ratzinger's: a thin blue robe hanging on a hook, a small fringed lamp on the bed stand and a few silver framed pictures of men in suits and women in wide dresses with massive flowers pinned to their shoulders. There was even a narrow brown comb waiting on the edge of the table.

"Mr. Ratzinger?" Nick whispered, but there was no answer, just faint breathing and the soft beep of the machines. Nick flipped off the TV, turning the room an inky dark, and turned to leave.

Mr. Ratzinger was sitting up in his bed, his figure illuminated by the machines.

"Sorry, Mr. Ratzinger. Thought you were sleeping. I'll flip the TV back on." Nick turned the heavy dial back on with a click, the screen filling with men in black suits and women in long, white dresses, endlessly swirling. "Okay. Good night then."

But Mr. Ratzinger didn't move to lay down.

"Are you sleepy?'

Mr. Ratzinger shook his head again. "M-music?"

Nick's eyebrows went up in surprise. It was the first time Nick had ever heard Mr. Ratzinger actually say anything.

"Do-do you want to help me with the music for the concert again?"

Mr. Ratzinger nodded vigorously and flipped the blanket off his skinny legs. He started to stand up, wobbled and fell back into the bed. Nick rushed forward to stabilize him, trying not to grip his skinny arm too hard. Under his hand, Mr. Ratzinger's bones felt like chicken wings.

Nick bit his lip. Maybe this wasn't a great idea. Carol was already pissed, though she'd been nice about it. And he couldn't risk being fired before he got that bonus.

"Hey, Mr. Ratzinger. How about we just…"

Mr. Ratzinger shook his head again and pointed to the dark corner of the room. Nick glanced over. There was a glimmer of silver. Nick squinted. Ah, yes. A wheelchair.

"Good idea, Mr. R. Let's get you situated, and we'll roll on out of here."

Back at his station, Nick set Mr. Ratzinger right next to the desk, adjusted his mask carefully over his nose and tucked a blanket around his legs for good measure. He took out his guitar, checking that the tuning held. He picked up his phone and pulled up his bookmarks.

"Okay," Nick said, setting his phone against the computer. "So I think I put together a pretty decent list, but you tell me what you think. Carol told me you were a singer."

Mr. Ratzinger paused, as if considering, and nodded.

"Right. So you get it." He strummed a few chords. Jesus. Why was he nervous? It was just a little old man in a ratty robe who probably didn't understand one word in five. Whose wife had just died. He probably didn't give a flying fuck about anything, let alone Nick's rusty ass playing. Nick coughed to clear his throat.

"Here we go."

The first chords of one of the Elvis covers filled the alcove. At the end, Mr. Ratzinger paused again, as if making a serious artistic determination, and again, nodded. Nick ducked his head and smiled, thanking God the mask hid most of his face. He started the next one and the next. They were all pretty straight forward chord progressions, but they sounded decent on the Yamaha, and his voice was okay, even though it was weird to sing through fabric. With his Taylor, he could really bring it home. And with Alex accompanying—

No. Shut it down. Nick flicked to the next song on his phone and brought the pick down hard on the first chord.

By the end of the set, Mr. Ratzinger bobbed his head a bit, maybe in approval or maybe just a side affect of whatever.

"So that's it," Nick said, flexing his chord hand. Man, he was soft. "What do you think?"

Mr. Ratzinger paused and shook his head.

"Look," Nick said, suddenly defensive, though again, who cared? "I know it's rough, but I'll put in some more practice."

Mr. Ratzinger shook his head again and grabbed at Nick's phone, hitting it off the desk.

"Hey!" Nick said, catching his phone before it hit the floor. "Jesus. Last thing I need is a cracked screen." Nick placed the phone carefully on the desk and deliberately slid it further away from Mr. R.'s surprisingly long reach. Mr. Ratzinger, his forehead more furrowed than usual, raised one shaky arm and pointed at the computer screen.

"M-moon," Mr. Ratzinger rasped, his voice muffled by the mask.

"Excuse me?"

"M-moon." Mr. Ratzinger pointed again.

"You mean that song from last night? I thought you didn't like it."

Mr. Ratzinger shook his head vigorously.

"So you do?"

Mr. Ratzinger nodded.

"I don't know. It's not really for solo guitar."

Mr. Ratzinger pointed to the computer again. "P-play. There."

Nick sighed. Sure. What the hell? "Okay. Let me see if I can find it." He clicked open the search engine and typed in Moon River 1961. On the page, he clicked on a lyric video and turned up the volume. It wasn't the same one. A breathy female voice over a soft guitar wafted out of the speakers. Well, this version wouldn't be too hard to play. Nick leaned in to listen.

But Mr. Ratzinger was shaking his head again, and tapped Nick's hand on the desk, almost hard enough to bruise.

"Okay, okay. I'll find the right one. Gimme a sec."

Nick clicked on the search engine again. Moon

River 1960s orchestra. The first result was the video from last night. He clicked on it, and the lush strings filled the small space again, even though the volume was pretty low. Mr. Ratzinger started breathing faster, his mask puffing in and out, and his eyes got even wider. Nick started to feel uneasy.

"Mr. Ratzinger, maybe I should—"

"No," Mr. Ratzinger said, as clear as could be and with more force than Nick thought he possessed in his whole body. "Please."

"Okay," Nick said and sat back in his chair. While the music played, he glanced at the second computer screen, checking the security cameras. You know, his job.

On the top corner, the window that showed the emergency exit at the end of the East hall, someone was standing by the doors. Nick sat up and squinted at the grainy picture. No, there was no one. Just the dark hall, dimly lit by the red exit sign.

The window went white, like it did sometimes, and then dark again, and Nick saw them. A person, in a white hospital gown, creeping down at the end of the hall near Mr. Ratzinger's room.

Goddamn it. If Carol found out he let another resident wander around at night unsupervised, she would kill him for sure.

"Hang on, Mr. R. I'll be right back."

Nick walked down the hall toward the exit. That far from his desk, the music echoed oddly off the tile walls, elongated and warped like someone was messing with the playback speed. It was disorienting, and Nick felt like the hallway was tipping a little, the slick linoleum sliding under his sneakers.

But when he got to the exit doors, there was nothing. No movement, all quiet, just darkness. And all the doors were shut, except Mr. Ratzinger's. It was so silent that he would have heard someone close or open a door.

Just in case, he peered into windows of nearby rooms, to see if anyone was moving, but everything was still. He checked Mr. Ratzinger's room last, but it was empty, of course, with the black and white movie still flickering silently on the walls.

Not sure what else to do, he peered out the glass of the exit door, to see if someone had gone outside, which was highly unlikely as it would have set off all sorts of alarms and the new emergency flood light besides. But the street behind the exit door glass was empty and slick after a late rain. A car went by, its high beams on. The beams momentarily blinded Nick in a harsh flash of white.

Must have been headlights. He recalled Mr. Ratzinger, who might have fallen over all by himself with no machines or support. The song had ended, the wing was completely quiet again. Nick quickly trotted back down the hall, his footsteps unusually loud on the linoleum.

Mr. Ratzinger was still upright, which was a relief. But when he turned to Nick, his eyes were damp with tears.

"Mr. Ratzinger! Are you feeling okay?"

"D-d… Daisy," Mr. Ratzinger said, and then something that Nick couldn't make out.

"Daisy, your wife, right?" Nick said slowly.

Mr. Ratzinger nodded and wiped roughly as his eyes with one gnarled hand.

"It's a nice song," Nick said, feeling like an idiot, but what else could he say? "Like for a wedding, right?"

"P-prom."

"Wow," Nick said again, completely at a loss. "Did you want to go back to your room?" Nick checked the large clock on the wall. "It's just past midnight."

"N-no," Mr. Ratzinger said. He lurched in the direction of Nick's guitar. "E-Elvis. Needs practice."

Nick snorted. "Dude. Everyone's a critic."

On the drive home, Nick thought about Mr. Ratzinger and that smarmy song. After he played the Elvis set, Mr. Ratzinger asked for "Moon" again, so he queued it up a couple of times, watching Mr. R. closely to make sure he didn't have a heart attack or fall over or anything. Now, even five hours after wheeling Mr. R. back to his room, the damned song was stuck in his head.

It was, no doubt, one of the cheesiest songs he had ever heard—sugary and loopy, with its full orchestra and no percussion, like the worst pop songs Alex used to make him listen to. But it meant something to Mr. R.

Nick turned on to one of the backroads leading to his apartment, the one that cut behind the warehouses on Route 309. This early in the morning, it was deserted and a little creepy. Glancing around the road, Nick pulled up his phone and did a quick search. "Moon River" came up. Nick glanced again at the road, making sure it was still empty in the grey pre-dawn light, and clicked on the song. Soft strings filled the car, and Nick put down his phone in the cup holder and looked back at the road.

A figure in white was directly ahead of him, giving him no time. He braked hard, the tires squealing and slipping on the wet cement.

Nick shouted, but it didn't matter. He went right through her.

Nick held on to the wheel as his car came skittering to a stop. For a second, he couldn't move his hands from the peeling leather, and his heart felt like it was trying to claw its way up his throat.

"Fuck!" he yelled. Did he hit her? Jesus, he had just taken his eyes off the road for a second, and she was there. Out of thin air, just standing in the middle of a backcountry road at the ass-crack of dawn. He started shaking.

Wait, wait, he thought. Check. He hadn't felt any impact. Maybe she jumped out of the way.

He killed the engine, the music running through the car's speakers cutting off mid-swoon, and turned around to look through the back of the car. The condensation on the windshield made it difficult to make out anything. With shaking hands, he pushed open his door and stood on legs that felt like he'd been up drinking all night. One of the car's alarms was dinging, but it sounded very far away. He checked the front of the car.

No blood, no dents. Nothing.

He turned around, looking the way he had come. Nothing. He could only have gone 50 feet or so from the … place where he saw her. But in the pre-dawn light, things were still mostly in shadow and there were no lights along this road. A light ground fog had gathered.

He had to go check.

He took an uncertain step and another.

"Hello? Hello?" he tried to call, but his voice came out rough and low. He couldn't seem to catch his breath. "Are you hurt?"

Jesus. What if she was so bad she couldn't talk?

What if she was dead? What if he'd killed her?

"Jesus, fuck," Nick said, but he kept walking. He should get his phone, call an ambulance. He didn't know what the fuck he'd do if he found her and she needed help.

He kept walking. "Hello?"

The sun was coming up quickly, burning off the fog. He looked to the left and the right, looking for anything on the damp, black road. Blood. A body. Skid marks. He kept walking until he reached the stop sign where he'd turned onto the road. He turned and walked back, looking along the shoulder, thinking that they could have gotten thrown off the road. But the ditches on both sides of the road were shallow and filled with weeds and beyond there were empty dirt fields going on for a while until ending in a scraggly tree line more than a thousand feet away. They couldn't have walked or crawled that far, could they?

Nick rubbed his eyes and tried to think. He hadn't heard an impact but there had been something there.

A someone. In white, a drapey sort of white. And a face, clearly, with two dark eyes. Or maybe two black sockets, where eyes should be.

Nick shook his head. It was lack of sleep. He'd only gotten three hours or so last night, staying up all night with his guitar and the songs. And the fog. It could have just been sun on the fog or the wet road. He walked back to his car and checked the Honda's hood for any damage. Nothing. Just the normal dings and scrapes from his crappy attempts at parking.

Yes, it had to be a trick of the fog or his mind or something. At least that made a lot more sense than a woman wearing white drapes in the middle of a back road at six a.m. who disappeared when a car went through her.

Nick had collapsed into bed as soon as he got home and slept like the dead until it was almost dark. He awoke as the streetlight outside his window came on, feeling more rested than he had in months. He still had a few hours before his shift, so he put on his mellowed out playlist, threw a frozen pizza in the toaster oven, and for the first time in months, pulled up the usual websites to see if anyone was looking for musicians again.

The news was grim. A lot of the places where Alex and he used to play were marked as permanently closed. Social media feeds looked bad, too. Everyone was announcing virtual concerts or posting dark

COVID memes. He clicked over to the Black Metal Coffee page and chuckled as he read Rosemary's obscenity laced posts. At least they were still in business, though they probably didn't need any help. Not that Nick had worked that job for the money. As a server, he always got his pick of performance slots.

He glanced at his phone. Almost seven on a Wednesday, and, per the website, the coffee shop closed at seven. Rosemary would probably be cleaning up. Before he could lose his nerve, he dialed the shop's number. She picked up on the first ring.

"Black Metal Coffee," crackled Rosemary's smoker voice.

"Hey, Rosemary. It's me—"

"Nick! Hun! How ya' doin'?" He could practically feel the force of her hug and smell her menthols through the speaker.

"Fine, Rosemary. Fine. You?"

"Oh, we're good, hun. Me and Cass can't complain. We're healthy, the girls are good, the shop is hanging in there... And with the vaccine news and that asshole finally out of the oval, the energy in the universe is about ready to shift, I tell you what."

Nick smiled. Rosemary seemed exactly the same. That had to count for something.

Well, there was no reason to wait. "So, I know it's late, but I was wondering if you knew of any place looking for music again."

"Sorry, hun," Rosemary said. "I wish I did. We still aren't letting anyone in here. Just meeting them at the door with their orders. It's painful not to play, you know? Like one of my arms is broken. How is Alex, by the way? You guys still working on that record?"

Nick swallowed hard. He could tell her, of course. Rosemary wouldn't judge him, he was pretty sure. But that would be a whole thing, probably. Better just to lie. "Oh sure. I mean, it's been strange. But we're getting there."

"Glad to hear it, hun. Everyone loved your music. I really think you have something there, Nicky. Very Elton and Bernie, right? Don't give it up."

"Sure. Look, Rosemary. I have to get ready for work."

"Sure, hun. Say hello to Alex for me. And we'll see you in 2021!"

Nick put down his phone and slid slowly down in the futon until he was lying flat on his back and pulled his sweatshirt over his head. Which was stupid. Who cared if he cried? There was no one to see him. He was alone, in his sad apartment, with his sad job and sad life, and no one cared, least of all him. For the millionth time, he thought about driving over to Alex's place. It was just on the other side of town, only a few blocks down the street past Glen Oak. She hadn't responded to his calls or texts since February and she'd blocked him on social media, but he could pull a John Hughes. Play some sappy love song on his car speakers. Refuse to leave until Alex came out and talked to him.

But that wouldn't do a goddamn thing, because he would have confirmed everything that she accused him of: that he was a selfish creep, just like all the other stupid guy musicians.

"You're a fucking bastard," she'd said, tiredly. They'd been standing outside in the driveway of Alex's parents house, arguing for an hour, the streetlight flickering on and off as the sun set.

"It was a mistake," Nick said. "I don't even know her name."

"Then why?" Alex asked. "Why the fuck would you do it?"

Nick didn't have the words to explain. Just that there was this clawing in him, all the time, and he had to do something to smash it. It was only months later, after Alex cut him off, that he could start to explain why, even to himself. That even when he was supposed to be at his happiest, playing music or even just with Alex, he was trapped in the realization that he would never be a famous musician, whether because of lack of talent or work ethic or just stupid luck. He'd pushed against that truth as hard as he could, but he couldn't get free or make it stop. So he did something shitty, trying to break free, knowing it was shitty the whole time.

Of course, it hadn't changed anything, except to make it all worse.

Nick pulled the sweatshirt off his face, flipped over on his side and stared at the opposite wall. He couldn't do this anymore. Every time he touched a guitar, he thought of his failed career and how he had hurt Alex. And it twisted up in his gut, guilt, shame and disappointment. He had to stop, completely. Music and his dreams were done. After this concert, he would take his bonus, sell his guitars and leave Pennsylvania. Go somewhere warm and cheap. Texas maybe. Get a job where no one got sick or died and he could turn off his brain completely. Maybe a convenience store, where he could just say, "Shop smart, shop S-mart" and not give a damn.

Yes, this would be the end. One last concert, and he would be done with it all. And if Mr. Ratzinger was the only person who showed up, that was fine with Nick. Because he didn't give a fuck anymore.

That night, Nick downloaded the rest of the chord progression onto his tablet in grim silence. He looked at his Yamaha and over at his Taylor. What the hell? If he was going to sell it, might as well get one final use out of it. He grabbed the Taylor and placed it gently on the floor in the Honda's backseat. He took the backroads slowly, looking out for walkers and animals and whatever else, but the streets were eerily empty all the way to Oak Glen.

At the guard desk, Carol was looking for a pen again.

"Hey ya, kid," she said. The crease was back and it was deeper than he'd ever seen it.

"What is it?"

"Mr. Ratzinger," she said. "He had another stroke."

A cold rush of guilt flashed over Nick's skin. Shit. Maybe his little midnight concerts had been too much for Mr. R. "Did—did something cause it?"

Carol shook her head. "Not really. His body is just giving out."

That should have given him some relief, but there was still a pit of dread in his stomach. He couldn't even talk to people without fucking them up.

"Is he... I mean, will he...?"

"It doesn't look good. He's been unconscious since morning."

"What about the hospital? Couldn't they help?"

"He's got a DNR, sweetie. And with COVID, it's safer for him here. We're meeting with the family tomorrow to discuss next steps."

Jesus. There was nothing but darkness. He glanced at the clock on the wall. For once in his life, he was a full twenty minutes early. "Do you mind if I sit with him for a while? I was practicing a song for him. I won't be late for my shift."

Carol paused and then nodded. "You're a good kid, Nick. Sure. Take as long as you like."

Nick's walk down to Mr. R's room seemed to stretch forever. The door was slightly ajar, and Nick pushed in before he could talk himself out of it. Someone had left the TV on again and it looked like the same old movie from the night before: men in black suits dancing with women in long white dresses, swirling around the screen in silence. Gray and white light flashed over the room, illuminating the empty bed and the slight shape of Mr. R. under a thin white blanket. A breathing machine wheezed.

"Hey, Mr. R.," Nick said, trying to sound cheerful and feeling like an absolute idiot. "Carol said you had a bad day."

No answer. Of course.

Nick set his guitar on the empty bed and pulled out one of the spindly plastic chairs from the wall.

"So I decided this concert is going to be my farewell tour," Nick said. "Now you've gone and cancelled on me." Nick glanced at his guitar and at the slightly open door. "Well, fuck it, how about a dress rehearsal?"

Gently, he shut the door and opened his phone to the song list. Damn it. He hadn't gotten a chance to tune. "Hang on a sec, Mr. R."

Nick opened the case and settled the Taylor in his lap, the wood feeling right in his hands. He gave a tentative strum. Actually, despite not being played for months, it wasn't bad at all, and the sound echoed warmly in the small room.

"Pretty good acoustics in here, Mr. R. You've been holding out on me. So, let's start from the top."

He started with his opening number, an older tune from the late 50s, keeping the volume as low as he could, though he knew that everyone in the wing could probably hear him and kick him out at any second. He transitioned into an Elvis medley, which he suspected was going to be a hit. He followed it with a slower number, a love song that wasn't too obnoxiously syrupy. Curling over his guitar, the neck vibrating against his palm, he could almost feel like he was back on stage at Rosemary's shop with Alex, playing to the usual crowd, imagining what it would be like when they played to thousands.

Almost. It wasn't like he got so lost in his set that he forgot that everything was fucked: that no matter what he did or how good he played, he was never going to be a professional musician, Alex was never going to speak to him, and Mr. R. was going to die. But for thirty minutes, he could hold that clawing feeling at a distance, outside, maybe even just beyond the glass windows of Mr. R.'s room.

When the last chord died away, he was met with silence and the beep beep beep of the machines.

This was ridiculous. Playing for a man who couldn't hear him and probably had no idea he was even there? Nick laughed a hollow, dry laugh. That, he guessed, summed up his entire musical career.

But the show must go on.

"Thank you," Nick said, acknowledging his nonexistent audience. "And now, as a special request for my old buddy Mr. R. and my final song of the evening, 'Moon River.'"

He pulled up the music he had found yesterday and strummed the opening G chord once. On the Taylor, the chord sounded fuller and rounder than the Yamaha. A swoony sound, but in a good way. He gripped the neck of the guitar and looked at Mr. Ratzinger. He was still, lying flat on his back, his eyes closed, his chest barely moving.

He's not even going to hear me. He's already gone. Nick bent down quickly, blinking his eyes clear, and strummed the opening G chord again. Nick started singing, his voice a little rough.

There was a sudden brightening in the room, and Nick glanced at the TV. But the screen was dark. He looked over to the bed, and his fingers slipped on the steel strings.

There, between the bed and window, was a white light, just hanging in the air. As Nick stared, the light elongated into a tall, thin figure. It leaned over Mr. Ratzinger's body, white skeletal arms reaching for him.

Nick gasped and dropped his pick. The figure turned to look at him.

It was the face from that morning: a white, empty face with black holes for eyes. Nick pulled back in his chair, the guitar falling to the floor with a horrible jangling sound. He knew he should run or yell or throw something, but he couldn't stand, like a great rock was sitting on his chest, and the white light was blinding. He held up one hand against the brightness and fumbled for Mr. Ratzinger's hand on the blanket.

"Mr. R. Don't worry. I'm here."

Abruptly, the light lessened. Nick pulled his hand away from his eyes. The figure was glowing, yes, but not as brightly, and Nick could see what he had thought was a grinning skull was the face of a young, completely ordinary woman. Her skin glowed with a blue-white light and her shoulder length hair and wide skirted dress danced around her like on some gentle breeze. Nick checked Mr. R., who seemed to be still breathing, and looked back at the woman.

She was looking at him, her face emotionless. She raised one transparent arm and pointed at Nick.

No. Not at Nick. At his feet, where the guitar lay on the floor. Nick pointed.

"Th-at?"

She—the ghost, because what the fuck else?—nodded.

Nick swallowed and picked up the guitar. He did one strum, and the A string popped. Shit, shit, *shit*.

"Sorry. One sec."

He pulled open the case. Did he have some extra strings? He hadn't checked before he left. What did a ghost do when you couldn't satisfy their demands? Take your soul? Fuck. Nick felt around on the side of the case.

There. In the side pocket. He pulled out the kit, his hands shaking. As quickly as he could, he removed the remnants of the broken string and popped the new one in. His fingers slipped a little as he wound the string around the machine head. The ghost waited patiently, like any bar goer when he and Alex had technical difficulties.

"Okay. Okay," Nick said, trying the chord. He was as nervous as he had been the first time he and Alex had played some of their originals at the coffee shop. Nick closed his eyes. That night, he had felt like he was going to throw up, and then it was fine and they played the most perfect set of their lives. What had happened?

That's right. He looked over at Alex, and she'd been grinning. "Let's fucking play," she mouthed at him.

Let's fucking play, indeed. He started to strum again.

The ghost bent its head softly and turned back to Mr. R. She reached—no, held out her arms—and her expression was pure happiness, as if there was no one in the world she wanted to see and nothing else she wanted to do.

Two strong hands reached up and clasped hers.

Out of the bed, unmasked and in a sharp suit and full head of hair that glowed blue-white in the dark room, climbed Mr. Ratzinger.

Nick reached the end of the song, his hands numb, and started again.

The ghosts started to dance, their motions as graceful as the figures on the TV. The room was filled with a sparkling energy, like light bouncing off a mirror ball. In his head, Nick saw Alex smile again, and for the first time, he felt the wall crack. Some of his anger and disappointment rushed out of him, like air escaping a balloon. It was a damned relief, and Nick felt his shoulders drop a little. There was still a core of sadness and regret that felt heavy inside of him, but that wasn't about Nick's failed career. Not really. It was about something more important. Someone who was the most important, and who Nick had deeply, probably irrevocably lost forever.

As Nick hit the last chord, the music drifted off into the air and so did Mr. Ratzinger and his wife, passing through the dark glass of the window, over the black lawn and out onto the dark road that glistened with rain. Mr. Ratzinger didn't look back. Why should he? He knew exactly what he needed to be happy.

The room slowly dimmed to darkness, the only sounds the white fuzz of the TV and the whine of an alarm. Nick was still hugging his guitar and crying when Carol found him.

It was late, we were tired, and neither of us were saying anything, just listening to the radio as we rode through the night. The moon was high, and there was fog lying low in the fields, but lower than the road which was slightly elevated.

We had just come out of a hairpin turn and started into the first straight stretch of road we'd seen in a while, when there he was. A man walking along the road.

He was at the far end of the stretch, perhaps a quarter mile distant. There were trees at the far end there, whose branches met as they crossed the road, forming what looked like the mouth of a tunnel. And this fellow was walking along just underneath them.

Now everyone has seen a person walking along the road at night. And that is just what this fellow looked like. His arms were swinging as he strode along. His clothing was nondescript...quite unremarkable. In fact, there was absolutely nothing strange about him at all, except for one thing. This man was not walking along the side of the road. He was walking in the middle of my lane. And he was making no efforts to move over!

Well, being the young wag that I was in those days, I was preparing to make some smart-alecky remark, like, "Well, if he doesn't get over, I guess I'll just have to run over his ass!"

But what I was also preparing to do is to slow down, move over into the oncoming lane, and assess the situation. Was this person drunk? Had he had an accident, was he hurt and needing help? Was he looking for trouble and going to throw a brick at us as we went past? I didn't know...but I didn't want to run over him accidentally if he fell over and I was going by too close and too fast.

But....

Before I could do either of those things...say my smart aleck remark or slow down and move over....

...this man began to float up into the air.

It was a slow and steady rise. His arms were still swinging and his legs still moving, but he was now going up instead of forward.

Every hair on my body stood at attention. My eyes were wide. My hands were tight on the wheel. I was doing everything I could to maintain a steady course. My body felt as though someone had touched two bare electrical wires to the base of my spine. Every muscle tight. I'm not certain I took a breath.

As we grew closer, he floated higher. Just before we got to the trees, he disappeared into the overhanging branches. We sped past underneath seconds later. I felt a tremendous chill. I looked back into the rearview mirror. I suppose I was looking to see if he would float back down.

He didn't.

After we left the cover of the branches and were a few yards further down the road, I looked over to my girlfriend.

"Did you see that?" I asked.

"Don't say anything, just get us out of here!" was her shouted sensible reply. I took that as a "Yes" and stepped on the gas.

We did not say a word the rest of the drive home. All the way, my brain was trying to process this new input. Rethinking what was possible in the world. The fact that when my grandmother and great grandmother told me their ghost stories that they purported to be true, perhaps they weren't JUST trying to make them a better story. Maybe they WERE true after all.

Months afterward, my girlfriend and I were talking on the phone, and I asked her about the incident...we had not spoken of it in all the time since.

"Say. That night driving back from Mount Saint Joe. What did you see?"

"I saw the same thing you did. A man walking down the road and he floated up in the air."

"Oh. That's what I thought."

Well, that incident opened my brain right back up again to what was possible in the world. And when you have an open mind, and perhaps just a touch of "the gift" as my grandparents called it...lots of things begin to present themselves. Like the forty years or so of stories I have experienced afterward.

-Owensboro, Kentucky. 1978.

The Girls of Blackthorn

Cadence Barrett

Victoria (1890)

Welcome to your bedroom in Hell.
It was a way of occupying my mind during my father's interminable, fiery sermons. "A lake of fire" is the way he usually described the tortures of damnation. But that description had always struck me as inadequate. Could Satan not devise a more creative version of Torment?

"Allow me to share with you a story that hangs heavy on my heart." Papa's countenance took on the studied grimness he assumed for these diatribes. "In a pauper's asylum, patients were, naturally, confined to their units at night. In the early hours a fire broke out on their ward. Many—in their state of confused reason—shrank away from the fire brigade. By the time they finally realized their error, the wall of fire was impenetrable." His gaze grew even more baleful. "A ghastly cry went up among the patients condemned to burn. Too late...*too late*...."

My father, I was convinced, was at heart a frustrated thespian.

Still. However melodramatically presented, a lake of fire could only remain interesting for so long.

If the Devil were as clever, as insidious and pernicious a presence in our lives as the good Reverend Parker maintained, he must be talented at inventing tortures for his victims: the non-Christians, the lapsed Christians, the not-good-enough Christians.

What would it be like to go to Hell? Waking to a new dwelling, a hostel or boarding house, perhaps. Satan would lead new arrivals on a tour, revealing the horror of their new domicile in increments, watching the last shriveled morsel of hope leaving their eyes as they realized the truth of their new dwelling place.

Perhaps the difference between the Hell room and a person's former, earthly home was subtle. A room, a narrow bed, a window. And only gradually, when you had been politely oriented, would come the creeping realization that something wasn't right. There was no wallpaper, and the painted walls were peeling, as if someone clawed them from within. The floor was littered with detritus. The mattress was soiled, the pillow dirty, infected; there was no earthly—or unearthly—possibility of laying your head on it. The window at first appeared to open onto something verdant: a garden, or at least trees. But as you drifted towards it, you saw that leaves and vines were growing through the cracks in the window frames, easing their way into the room as if trying to reclaim it.

The odd thing was that Satan brought you to your room cordially and with the utmost politeness. You were momentarily diverted by his charm and grace.

"The Devil," my father claimed, "is never more subtly himself than when he appears clothed as an Angel of Light."

But when you are left alone in your new room—your eternal bedchamber—it slowly dawns on you: you are surrounded by darkness.

Will you be left alone in this room forever? A place you can never escape, not even through the mortal sin of suicide, which would just bring you back here?

Beyond Papa's sermons, I thought no more about my iteration of Hell. It wasn't until I stepped over the threshold of Blackthorn Asylum that I recalled my youthful, imaginative forays into a bedchamber in Perdition.

Because now, I saw my own vision arrayed before me in all its desiccated horror, wings and staircases and dim corridors and dank rooms.

And two hatchet-faced matrons, possessing none of the beauty and grace with which I had gifted my imaginary Lucifer, ushering me into its depths.

Doreen (2015)

Blackthorn Asylum, just outside of town, was shut down around the time I started first grade. It stood empty and moldering on its ten-acre plot, the preferred destination for thrill-seeking high school kids.

I was one of them, along with my boyfriend, Danny. We circled the buildings on foot, the whole thing a dark heap that seemed to exude bad intentions, scaring ourselves into a panicky retreat. I was so unsettled that, once inside Danny's car, all I wanted was to smoke weed and have sex, in that order.

I'm pretty sure Troy was conceived in Danny's car in the Blackthorn parking lot.

I was finishing at community college when Blackthorn reopened, rebranded as a hospital instead of an asylum. I was impressed the first time I saw it after the renovation, with the building restored to its former Victorian awesomeness. But it didn't take away from the weird feeling that hung over the hospital and its grounds. I picked up on the strangeness right away when I went for my interview.

They were advertising for a mental health technician. I wasn't sure exactly what that was, even after googling it. In the CareerBuilder ad they said a high school diploma was required, but an associate degree was "preferred." So I figured my degree would be worth something to them even though I suspected they wished it were in psych, not English.

The pickings were slim in Hayfield, though, in terms of young people staying in town after they got their college degrees. I knew they'd most likely take what they could get.

The Blackthorn job was a whole new thing for me. Before that, I'd only worked at a convenience store in town. That first night, after I got home and put Troy to bed, my mom asked how it went.

"Okay, I think." I shrugged. "Seems like an interesting job."

"Interesting good, or…?"

"I was bored out of my mind at McCarthy's, so I guess good."

To tell the truth, it was a mixed bag. There were positives. I liked the feeling of being challenged. On my first day I'd learned to use a blood pressure machine and to read urine drug screens. I learned how to navigate our computer program. I took folks outside for smoke breaks and kept myself available to anyone who needed to talk.

Later in the week I started running morning check-in. Eventually, they said I'd be facilitating psychoeducation groups too.

I thought I'd probably made the right decision by coming here. It was the first time I ever felt challenged on a job. I mean, how challenged can you be at a convenience store?

In quiet moments, though, which there weren't many of, something about the hospital bothered me.

Maybe it was because I'd been here before. The place was immaculate now, the brick façade stained and painted, inside walls whitewashed, paintings hung all around and new Ikea-type furniture in all the common rooms.

But there remained an—*undertone*—that crept up on me.

It was different on various shifts at Blackthorn. The early shift was great. On the four to midnight, though, I felt a misery gathering in the air. You didn't need a history of mental illness to recognize depression when you walked face-first into a cloud of it. It ambushed me in certain places: specific hallways, and on rainy days when I walked the tunnels between my unit and the cafeteria.

After work, I'd roll down the windows to let the wind play through the front seat of my Ford Taurus, blaring my music until I'd shaken it off. I didn't want to take it home with me.

Victoria

"Good morning, Miss Moral Insanity."

It was Matron Russell's standard greeting. She had gotten hold of my chart and informed me, smug with malice, of my diagnosis.

On this particular morning, a week since my admission to the asylum, she was winding herself up and going strong by six-thirty.

"Miss Apprehended, is it?" she said. "Or are we Miss Construed today?"

Her worst quality in my eyes—besides her cruelty—was her exaggerated assessment of her own education.

I clenched my jaw. I had been given to shooting pains in my head since my arrival at Blackthorn, for no doubt this reason.

"Do you actually know the meaning of those words?" I asked.

"Too clever for your own good," she rejoined, and scraped up against my shoulder, an unnecessary swipe. I thought she meant to pass me, but she leaned in close and blasted her foul breath in my face. I grimaced and turned away from her, but her scorching whisper landed in my ear: "Strumpet. Bagtail." I set my face in stone; even after a week her vile insults hadn't ceased to sting. "A married man's doxy, is what I heard."

Dollymop. Whore. I closed my mind to the memory.

"Fortunately, you'll never have to worry about *your* virtue," I rejoined. "With that gibface of yours, your maidenhead is entirely safe."

She took my face in her hand and dug her fingers into my jaw, sending a jagged pain through my ears. "What was that, Parker? Say it again."

Her fingers gripped so hard that tears sprang to my eyes. "Get off me," I gritted out.

"I'll oblige you on that, slut." She raised her voice to summon another matron. They moved away, put their heads together and spoke in tones too hushed for me to hear.

A small warm hand furtively encased one of mine. I turned to find an elderly lady sitting next to me. After a moment I recognized Miss Owens, who slept in the cot next to mine.

"You must go to Matron Russell and apologize," she whispered.

I squeezed her hand in return to acknowledge the wisdom of her direction.

I knew I should apologize. Mentally I excoriated myself for my lack of discipline. It was what had landed me in this hellhole. But Miss Russell's words—*strumpet, bagtail, wagtail*—left me raging. Because I supposed on some level they were true.

Scarcely half an hour had passed when both matrons came for me.

"Get up, tart," Miss Russell addressed me. I slowly stood, understanding that it would go worse for me should I appear non-compliant. They took me to a room containing eight rusted, unclean freestanding tubs, and I saw immediately what they had prepared for me: a freshly drawn ice bath.

"No!" I tried to back away when I saw it. Due to my unfashionably thin frame, I was already always cold. Immersion in an ice bath would be akin to torture.

"Take off all your clothing. Including your underthings," Miss Russell ordered, stone-faced.

The ice bath was even worse than I'd imagined; it was so frigid that the water seemed to burn my skin. Even worse, a heavy muslin was placed on top of the bath and I was strapped in, with only my head spared from immersion.

Desperately I attempted to detach myself from my

physical circumstances, with initial scant success. But as the afternoon progressed to evening, and I knew myself to be abandoned to the gelid waters and the darkness, my mind did indeed seem to split off from my body, slowly dividing itself from my flesh. Eventually I was able to cast back to an earlier time in my life, and to escape into it.

I had gone from being considered a hoydenish tomboy as a child to a bluestocking in my young teens, a sobriquet I claimed proudly. But puberty brought its own set of issues. By age fourteen I'd amassed a secret cache of dime novels. One did not read these books for their literary content; I was seeking stimulation of an entirely different sort. Though I had been severely, if obliquely, instructed about the dangers of onanism, it was the only way to satisfy unbearable longings. Reading about the *sweet death* didn't have a patch on actually experiencing it.

This was my only avenue for release of lustful impulses, until the advent of Mr. Chandler when I was sixteen.

Mr. Chandler was our French and German tutor. My aptitude for languages seemed to impress him; I was granted advanced lessons in these subjects, long after my sisters were dismissed from the classroom.

My reaction to Mr. Chandler—*Richard* when we were alone—affected me so intensely that I became awkward and clumsy in his presence. I barely dared meet his eyes. When he placed a hand on my shoulder to signify pleasure at my scholarly acumen, I could feel my face go hot.

When Richard kissed me for the first time, the sensation was a river of delight rippling through my body, bringing me close to the state I had heretofore achieved only through the forbidden act of onanism.

Emboldened by my eagerness, he asked me to meet him for a midnight picnic. He said he had no expectations of me, but I knew that if he tried to make love to me, I might easily succumb to his seduction, so great was my attraction to him.

We met three times. Those nights are burned into my memory as among the highlights of my life. There are times I regret surviving our final tryst; times when I wish that sweet death had been a real one.

My gravest error came when I wrote Richard a letter and left it on his desk in the schoolroom. Through the worst imaginable turn of events, the missive fell into the hands of my father.

How is it possible to describe the terror I felt when Papa summoned and confronted me? He berated me in terms I knew from books but had never heard actually spoken in society: harlot, dollymop, tart, doxy, whore. More than one sort of whore in fact; at one point he called me the Scarlet Whore who sits on the seven hills of Rome; then he called me a hedge whore; referring, no doubt, to the picnics.

He proceeded to give me his opinion of Mr. Chandler: he was a blackguard, a villain, a knave who had seduced me with his "whore pipe."

When Papa got going, as in the pulpit, he became truly invested in his subject. One might even say he relished this one.

He quoted lines from my letter. *Our beautiful lovemaking* became "a perverted, diseased rant which would have caused any book to be burned which included it."

He finished by saying, with a calm that frightened me more than any violence would have done, "I have obviously dismissed the despicable reprobate, and threatened him with gaol if he ever approaches you again. Moreover, I have told him I am still considering whether or not it is my duty to inform his wife of his treachery."

His wife. The words tore through my body; my mind, initially, could not absorb their meaning. Tears leapt into my eyes, and I turned my face away, but not before Papa saw the misery imprinted on it.

"Oh, you didn't know about his wife, did you?" he pursued. "Or his three children? In all the languages you spoke together, he was clearly too—occupied with your education—to bother informing you about such an irrelevant detail." He drew back, surveying me like some distasteful insect. "I am still considering your punishment. Nothing that comes readily to mind is in any wise sufficient to address your monstrous actions. You fully deserve a beating to within an inch of your depraved life, but I don't know whether I can bring myself to touch you sufficiently to administer it."

Now my tears ran freely. The threat of a whipping made me blanch with fear, since I had never in my life been struck. But the understanding that Papa considered me too low and dirty to even touch in violence sliced me like a scalpel, from throat to belly.

"You have never taken part in my life or my moral education," I said, "not beyond your hateful sermons. You have neglected all of us and devoted yourself entirely to your religion."

Now in his pale, icy eyes I saw that I had hit my target because he knew my words were true. I saw something then, a hint of remorse, a memory of a time we'd been close. The gap could have been bridged; I saw him softening and felt a responsive melting in myself. But his eyes flashed, as if with a new thought.

"*My* religion?" He stepped forward; I involuntarily withdrew a step. "Tell me, daughter. Is it not *your* religion also?"

This confounded me. I scarcely knew what I believed these days. I had studied other religions, Mohammadanism, Hinduism, Oriental Orthodoxy; I had also read, with interest, tracts written by agnostics and atheists. Stumped, I blurted the truth: "I don't know what my religion is. Or if I even have one."

At this he slapped me, so hard my vision was jarred out of focus. He took me by the shoulders and pushed me roughly against the wall.

"You will kneel and ask God's forgiveness for your unbelief. Your whoredom. Your prurience. Your filthy mind. I don't know if God can forgive you, but your only hope now is to implore Him for mercy."

"I don't want mercy from any God in whose likeness you were created. I loathe God." I hurled the words at him. In my desperate search for something that could hurt him, I suddenly remembered *Die froeliche Wissenschaft*: "God is dead!"

I fully expected him to beat me bloody. But he stepped back and dropped his hand. The horror stamped on his visage caused me instant remorse.

But a stubbornness took hold of me. I would not beg his forgiveness, or God's. I loved Richard, though in his perfidy it was now clear he did not love me back.

"I do not—I do not know what to say to you." Papa's words emerged with an uncharacteristic feebleness. "Leave me. I do not want to see you. Until I tell you otherwise, you are confined to this house. You are not to address me, or even to glance in my direction should we be forced to occupy the same room or pass in the corridor." He turned and walked to the door; after opening it, he held it for me, with a parting salvo:

"You are no longer my daughter."

Doreen

The 3-11 shift turned out to be my favorite. I could give Troy breakfast, hang with him all morning, take him with me if I had errands. At two-thirty I left for work, and Mom or Danny had him for the rest of the day, until his bedtime. Which with my mom was ridiculously early and with Danny ridiculously late, but we all had to learn to roll with the punches.

It rained for a week solid in October, and I took the underground tunnels to the cafeteria every day. When I went there at night, I felt that sense of presence, like having somebody near me—behind me or just to my right, but out of view, like a blind spot.

I told Maisy, one of the case managers, how the tunnels creeped me out, and she offered to come with me. "We usually team up if we can," she explained. "None of us wants to go alone."

It turned out that most of the staff had felt or seen odd things at night in the hospital. For myself I just continued to sense that hovering presence in the tunnel. Not benevolent.

Four months after starting at Blackthorn, I had to stay two hours late because the unit was short-staffed. As I tumbled into my car to drive home, I opened a can of Pepsi to stay awake on the drive, turned up the radio, and rolled down the driver's side window.

About a quarter of the way down the drive, the sight of something white loomed up ahead of me at the side of the road.

At first it appeared amorphous. As I drew closer, slowing my car in some alarm, I saw that the pale thing was a person, a woman dressed in something resembling a hospital gown, but longer. The woman's hair was waist-length and matted in back. She was running swiftly, her gown flying behind her. There was something strange—off—about the tableau, but also a sense of wild joy, a feeling of freedom that was almost palpable.

My first thought was that it might be a patient, escaping AMA. There were two kinds of patients: those that had been sectioned, and those on a voluntary hold, who signed a statement stipulating that they could check themselves out at will. But even those needed to give a 72-hour notice first.

Either way, they didn't get to just up and leave in the night.

I accelerated to catch up with her. As I approached, she glanced over her shoulder, seeming to get a glimpse of me, but turned around again.

I put on my high beams, but she didn't turn.

When I pulled up beside her, I called out through my open window, "Hey! Can I help you?"

Without seeming to hear me, she cut off the path, fleeing into the tree-studded landscape of the hospital grounds. Quickly, she was absorbed into the night.

I parked, got out of my car, and yelled out again. "Hello! Why are you running?"

No response. I thought of following but I could no longer see her, and the whole area was quiet.

I pulled out my phone and called security, then my unit. A hospital-wide check on all patients would be instigated.

Nothing more I could do. I took another swig of soda, unwrapped a Kind bar, and did my best to stay awake on the drive home.

The next day, when I came in at three, I learned that all the patients were accounted for. No one had gone missing in the night.

Victoria

After six years at Blackthorn, I had never transcended my fear of certain "therapies." Hydrotherapy was among them. Electrical stimulation, not introduced until my second year at Blackthorn, proved even worse.

"It's painless, Miss Parker," the nurse-matron—pretty, genteel Mrs. Crain—assured me, attaching the electrodes to my fingertips.

I was trembling and perspiring with fear. With her characteristic gentleness—which, I must add, was highly *un*characteristic of Blackthorn staff—she placed a hand on my shoulder, smoothing back my long rope of hair which had, as always, escaped from its plait.

"Now look at me," she instructed. "Keep looking into my eyes. I assure you, you are safe."

I screamed when the current electrified my body; it was by far the worst pain I'd ever experienced.

"Hush," Mrs. Crain said, softly, as if reassuring a child who'd sustained some negligible injury. "It doesn't hurt as much as all that."

Tears flooded my eyes. "Yes, it damned well does—"

I began, but I cut my own words short with a second scream, as she sent another jolt of electricity through my body.

Her face hardened slightly, as did her eyes, locked with mine; but she never broke her air of smug sorrow as she closely watched me.

Wracked by sobs, I drew in ragged breaths, barely able to speak, but I managed to challenge her: "Is this what you call 'moral treatment'?" But the words had scarce escaped my lips before a third jolt pierced me with its jagged current.

I knew I was going to die, without having any time to prepare myself. And Mrs. Crain's lovely, evil face was the last thing I was to see before leaving life behind.

When I came awake, I was aware of a pounding headache, and there were tears on my face. After the initial plunge into darkness, I had dreamed of being young again, skating with my sisters on the pond behind our house.

Once I had been young and happy and free. It was hard to believe now.

Amazingly, though, I discovered that I possessed an ability to pry my consciousness from my body under their tortures. I would stare up into a corner of the ceiling, fiercely concentrating my energy on that spot. I did this doggedly even when in pain, until my spirit successfully swarmed to my point of fixation.

Usually, I returned to my past as I dissociated, to happier times, when Mama was alive and Papa not so stern, when I had my sisters around me. It was a gift to relive those memories—simple times whose wondrous happiness had somehow escaped my notice at the time of their occurrence.

In my seventh year at Blackthorn, something unexpected, and wonderful, finally happened: Papa came to visit me. When I met him again, I was shocked by how much he had aged. From his expression, I imagined he felt the same degree of shock at my reduced condition.

At first, we were awkward with each other, both fumbling for words. I was astonished when his veined, tremulous hand found mine and covered it.

"Forgive me, daughter," he said. His voice was pitched low and lacked its old resonance, emerging from his throat as if cracked over a bed of sharp stones. "I should have visited you earlier."

My eyes riveted themselves to the floor. "Why did you not?"

"Dr. Meredith advised me it would likely unsettle you."

I felt my face close like a fist. "That is what they tell the families, so they can avoid scrutiny. They are forced to do a great deal of work to clean and rearrange things every time someone's loved one comes to visit."

"Do you believe you should come home, Victoria?" he asked. I could scarce credit the openness in his eyes; he was actually deferring to me.

"I want that above all else." My heart had started to leap in my chest, like a wild animal behind its cage of ribs.

"Then it shall be," he said. He assured me he would try to have me released by the year's end.

Within two months, though, before he could bring his plan to fulfillment, I received word that Papa had suffered a hemorrhagic stroke, which within five days proved fatal.

It was a strange sort of loss for me to suffer. I mourned him, I mourned the relationship we may have finally had a chance to redeem. But more than all else, it was a coffin lid slamming down hard over my hopes.

I took the only avenue left to me. I fled.

It was under cover of darkness, in the late October of my eighth year at Blackthorn, that I slipped from my bed, traded my nightdress for my white, faded-print cotton uniform, and purloined the key chain that hung on Miss Cassett's chest as she slept after her usual overindulgence in beer, and slipped into the darkness outside.

It was dawn before they found me, after a most strange night, filled with alternating exhilaration and terror. I ran down the long, winding path that connected Blackthorn to the main road, the wind beating my long skirt, picking up my unbound hair; I felt myself a wild thing, part of the forest, electrified by a sense of the freedom I'd not experienced in years. I felt like a bat, a bird, a part of the wind and the night world; yet at the same time, I knew they were in pursuit of me, and I knew terror.

I had a hastily cobbled-together plan to make it to the nearest large city, where I could mingle in an incognito state. I could become a street supplicant, begging for money in a metropolitan area, until I managed to think of some other way to earn my keep.

I was gone from Blackthorn for a full twenty-four hours before I was caught and brought back. I fought so fiercely they used excessive force in trying to subdue me: gagging me, binding my arms behind my back, and bashing me about the face.

I fully expected upon my return to be immersed in another ice bath or wrapped in wet hot towels and strapped into my bed, a somehow even worse fate. Instead, they put me inside an instrument of torture: a strait waistcoat. They then enhanced my punishment, placing me, thus confined, into a "padded room."

The confinement of the strait-coat was bad enough; but when I was thrust into the tiny, featureless room, I became subject to a strange sensation, mingling unbearable confinement and limitless space. Quickly, it became like a heap of giant stones upon which my skull was split open and my brains were dashed. I had, at once, the perception of being smaller than the tiniest flea, yet so large I could not even fit within the room, but was pouring out of myself, a formless void, into every corner. I tried to shut my eyes against this sickening feeling, but that only worsened it.

After I had exhausted myself struggling and screaming, I finally fell back limp, exhausted. The room was still spinning around me; or rather I, with my formless form, was churning within it. I tried to calm myself and find a corner of the ceiling as a point of fixity. Though I could barely discern up from down, I chose a spot arbitrarily and fixed my gaze upon it.

Finally, the room's whiteness ceased to beat like a merciless sun upon my eyes; the light darkened, with nightfall or the invention of my own imagination, I could not tell. But it made my meditation easier. With my mind emptied of its usual scurrying, unproductive chatter, I was able to see an expanded horizon. I tried, and at the same time did not try, to see beyond the pale.

When my consciousness finally surrendered, it was like stepping from the shore into the ocean. I was immersed in some vast new crucible: dreaming, yet fully awake.

I knew at once I was still at Blackthorn, in an operating room. On the table, an older man had been strapped down by leather bindings across his ribcage, securing his arms to the bed, with another brutal-looking strap just above his knees.

A number of people surrounded him. I counted at least three gentlemen wearing white coats, stethoscopes hanging around their necks. There were nurses as well, clothed in a uniform the likes of which I had not seen before, dresses with pinafores, and uncomfortable-seeming caps on their heads. Other people stood back farther from the table; they appeared to be hospital officials.

The eldest of the three physicians held an apparatus to the patient's head. The bound man's eyes were those of a trapped wild creature, alive with terror. Two rounded instruments were placed against the sides of his head. Obviously, he knew what was coming; I saw tears escaping form the sides of his eyes, while his lips moved in a silent, desperate prayer.

The sight of an old man being reduced to such helpless terror was dreadful.

When the electrical stimulation was applied to his head, I jumped along with the patient. I knew, from having electrodes attached to my fingers, how the sensation burned and jolted. But this appeared a thousandfold what had befallen me. The patient's body convulsed grotesquely. His unnatural jerking, his white-foaming mouth, was horrible to see.

It seemed unspeakable that any person—especially a medical doctor—could set out to deliberately inflict such violation upon another.

The intensity of my emotion—my horror and repulsion—seemed to catapult me out of the spell. I jerked, as one does in a light sleep to the sensation of falling, and found I had returned to my own torture chamber, the room of infinite space and coffin-confinement.

Before, my forays had catapulted me into the past, into beautiful memories of innocent times.

This new vision was certainly no throwback memory. It did not seem to be even of the present day. The nurses' clothes were so strange. They were clearly uniforms, nonetheless the skirts were shorter than any I had ever seen worn by a lady, or even a skivvy.

The idea that the future could be even darker than the present troubled me greatly. I spoke of it to the asylum alienist, who took notes, sagely nodded, and offered a sensible though limited and in my view, incorrect interpretation: I clearly had lost all hope in the future, both for myself and the world at large.

I also told Miss Owens, my bunkmate, whose black-hearted children, I'd learned, had confined her to this place when her melancholy grew intolerable for them. Miss Owens believed me. Why should she not? This place was evil enough now; there was no reason to believe it would self-correct on its dark course into the future.

After my flight, the Medical Director prescribed morphine, mixed into a draught of brandy, for my perturbed mind, to be given me at bedtime. I welcomed the few hours of relief it granted me nightly.

Doreen

In the weeks following that first sighting, I didn't see the girl in white again. But working the 3-11 shift, I sometimes saw, or sensed, other inexplicable things. It usually happened toward the later part of the evening.

Approximately one month after I'd seen the woman in white running down the road in front of the hospital, I saw her again. It was following a shift that once again lasted two hours later than usual, and I was so tired I almost couldn't see straight. The figure looked over her shoulder as my car approached, and then cut off the road into the woods and disappeared.

This time I didn't call anyone.

Victoria

As time wore on, I fought not to lose myself.

Days, weeks and months stretched into an abyss of emptiness. I sat in common rooms surrounded by women who gibbered, women who muttered, women whose minds were utterly clear but who were cast down in depression, abandoned by husbands, by adult children, by parents who found their eccentricities too vexing to tolerate.

I took up my studies of French and German again and was able to practice the latter with a new admission to the hospital, Frau Schmidt, who spoke no English. In return for helping me regain fluency in German, I tutored her.

No matter how I tried to fill my time, though, boredom remained an unending passive torment. Still, there were always exponentially more vicious modes of torture practiced upon us as well. With my rebellious nature and probing inquiries, I was often subject to their torturous methods of "discipline."

Subjection to these punishments led to the honing of my one escape valve: the ability to fixate on one corner of the ceiling, which produced a new phenomenon: my voluntary departure from the misery of my circumstances into the outside world, an ability I began to refer to as "traveling."

My friends on the ward perceived my sorrow and sense of waste. Miss Owens tried to raise my spirits. Minna and Lilly, two ladies imprisoned at the will of church-elder relatives, joined her and asked me to recount the vision of the old man whose torture I had somehow seen. Accordingly, I enlightened them.

"I believe I have seen the future of this place," I said. I didn't know exactly why I believed this so firmly, except that the visions had been so detailed—down to the absurdly short nurse uniforms that showed their ankles—and that my imagination, while creative enough, was not so finely honed as to invent new fashions and a sadistic medical orthodoxy.

My asylum friends knew me well enough to trust the bedrock of my sanity, even as my visions multiplied. I saw a girl whose teeth had all been removed after her doctors evidently concluded they were the source of her madness; when this produced no change, they began to cut out her internal organs. I saw a child who was restrained as a doctor thrust a sharp, pointed object through the top of his eyelid into his brain, assuring the parents this would cure his maladjusted behavior.

My friends eagerly drank in the details of my visions, which depictions soon spread through the wards.

My capacity to escape the asylum strengthened over time. When subject to isolation or confinement, I took to traveling out the front door in my mind, and into the surrounding ten acres of woods owned by the asylum.

I learned to project myself—not even into the trance-like state that produced my visions—but simply into flight, my gown fluttering about my wrists and ankles, hair unbound and lifted on the wind, swift like an antelope or a brown hare.

The odd thing, though, was that even in my imagination I could not pass beyond the stone wall that circled the asylum.

This incapacity reminded me of a game I had played with myself as a girl: trying to turn around in a full circle in my mind while physically standing still. I could never manage it. I would turn around halfway, to the point of facing backwards; but I could not push myself farther. There was something tight in my psyche, tethering me too closely to my corporeal being.

Now it appeared I was tethered to Blackthorn.

One night in October of the year 1899, when I had been at the asylum nine years, I had an exceedingly strange experience while traveling.

The first anomaly I noticed as I ran was a light flooding me from behind, and an unusual sort of noise, a purring, but low, almost a grinding sound. I looked back over my shoulder to glimpse a horseless carriage gaining on me.

This alone did not come as a stunning surprise. I was aware that hydro-carbon carriages had come on the market in the mid-1890s, reserved of course for the very few who were both modern and wealthy.

But when the thing stopped beside me, a young woman emerged from the chauffeur's side, clearly seeing me, and somewhat alarmed by the sight. She herself seemed a curious-looking creature. Her blouse was short-sleeved, with some kind of thermal undershirt covering her arms to the wrists beneath it; she wore purple trousers made of the same flimsy appearing material.

I had never in my life seen a woman clothed in trousers.

I hid in the woods when she noticed me. This being the first time that anyone I saw in a vision or projection could actually see *me*, it gave me quite a strange turn.

I was oddly excited to see the same young woman during my next projection. This time, in early evening, she was entering the last unit I'd inhabited. I wondered: if I followed her onto the ward, would she see me again?

But not this time: I clearly remained incognito, as if my desire for invisibility brought about its own fulfillment.

The unit was so changed from the reality of my own experience that I could scarcely credit it as the same edifice that held me imprisoned in 1899. There were no candles or oil lamps in evidence. The lighting was bright, almost blinding to my eyes.

But it was the cleanliness that most astonished me. From the nurses' desk to the lobby where a group of people congregated, everything appeared spotless, and smelled, if not wonderful, then at least medicinal.

I grew bolder and followed the young woman to the nurses' station.

"Hey, Doreen," one of the patients called out as she passed, "how are you?"

My young woman—Doreen, apparently—smiled. "Fine, y'know, just living the dream."

The patient emitted a cackling laugh. "I told you what *fine* means."

"I forget," Doreen said. "Tell me again, Michele."

"Fucked-up, insecure, neurotic, and emotional." Another cackle.

Doreen smiled, as if tickled by this piece of impertinence. "That's me," she said. "'Nailed it."

This left me so astonished my thoughts were in a tangle. In my experience, the matrons and even the nurses were often creatures of low breeding and minimal education, and they frequently cursed at us like stevedores. But for one of *us* to curse at *them*—it was unheard of—we would have been dreadfully punished.

I trailed Doreen for what seemed hours. She took patients' vital signs; sat with them in a large circle to discuss the day they had just spent; accompanied them to another building for dinner; and supervised their "smoke breaks." Finally, she rounded them up before bedtime to stand in line for their nightly doses of medication—all in pill form, I noticed, no draughts. It did not seem that any patients were given beer or brandy, which I found odd.

When the unit was quiet, Doreen lingered at the nurses' station. One of the nurses, an older woman, looked up at Doreen's approach. "How's Troy?" she asked.

"Oh my God," Doreen said, "the terrible twos. He's discovered swearing now." But she said it with a smile, as if amused despite herself. "And my mom goes, well, who do you think he gets *that* from?"

The nurse raised her eyebrows.

"I know." Now Doreen's tone was sheepish. "I've gotta watch my mouth around him. They're little sponges."

"It's a different world," the nurse replied. I noticed that she had rather a sour face. "When I was growing up, any girl who got pregnant HAD to get married."

Doreen screwed up her features. "You say that like it's a good thing."

"Well, you know, parents were stricter back then. They insisted you give babies a name."

"Oh my God." Now Doreen was laughing. "I just can't. Troy *has* a name, it's Perry. It was always good enough for me."

At this point I was stunned. My concentration evaporated and I found myself back in my own Blackthorn, shivering under wet cold sheets.

What on earth sort of world had I found my way into? Was it a true glimpse of things to come, or a product of my fevered mind?

I began laughing. Perhaps I was "FINE." I must have been hysterical at that point, because I began cackling to myself. I repeated Michele's words aloud: *Fucked-up, insecure, neurotic, and emotional.*

That did, rather frankly, sum it up.

It was fully a month later that I found myself outside Blackthorn asylum again. I had fixed my concentration on a ceiling corner in a state of utter fatigue, having exhausted myself struggling against my bonds.

When I opened my eyes, I found myself, to my own astonishment, in the woods near the gravel road leading to the main gate. I closed my eyes, shivered in delight at sensing the wind in my hair, fluttering my ragged skirt, bathing me in the scents of growing things.

I awaited Doreen's arrival, but it did not seem imminent. Finally, I approached the building, hoping that for a second time my presence would go unperceived.

The same proceedings unfolded as they had during my last visit; but this time, I saw someone who was dressed neither in the strange nurse/matron uniform, nor in the even stranger, exceedingly casual attire of the patients.

From a corridor in a hallway where I had not yet ventured came a dark-haired, dark-complected woman, clearly not of European origin. I could not place her race classification exactly; she might have come from some region in Asia, or the Middle East.

But she carried herself as if she held a station superior to both matrons and nurses. For one thing, she wore what appeared to be her own clothes, a kind of business suit with trousers, setting me off on a tangent of curiosity as to whether any women wore skirts in this world. Her trousers were well-pressed, her blouse crisp and well-tailored, her shoes clearly expensive black leather.

One of the nurses turned at her entrance. "Dr. Wright, hi, I didn't know you were still here."

Doctor Wright?

Not only a female: a non-Caucasian female. I stared at her in fascination. Was it truly possible that things could ever change to this extent?

It was her next words, however, that completely staggered me. "Well, I'm off for two days now," she said. "I'm arranging a retirement party for my wife. It's a lot more work than I'd imagined."

Her wife.

Her *wife*.

I studied her to make certain she was in reality a

female. Despite her severe clothing and trousers, there could be no doubt of her gender.

She was a woman in middle years. With a wife.

I looked to the two nurses at the station, trying to ascertain whether either of them showed signs of shock. Neither appeared to find anything untoward, or even particularly interesting, in the doctor's words.

And to think that I had been accused of "Moral Insanity."

Doreen

I'd been working at Blackthorn for almost a year when I started suspecting I was pregnant again. There was a certain kind of queasiness I'd experienced in my first pregnancy; also, my breasts and my back hurt, and I was unreasonably tired. On work nights, it was even harder now to stay awake in the last hour, when the patients were in bed and the unit was mostly quiet.

One night I practically staggered out to my car. The night air did wake me up a bit, though, to the point where at least I knew I was safe to drive. Just to be sure, I munched on a bag of chocolate-covered espresso beans I kept in the glove compartment.

I was about halfway down the drive when I saw her again—the white of her raggedy dress with its faded pattern showing up at a slight distance in my headlights. She paid me no attention this time, but picked up her pace so that the spring breeze caused her skirt to flow behind her like a sail. She seemed to be headed, in a determined manner, to the front gate.

As I drew near, she stopped and turned her head.

It was the first time I'd seen her up this close. She was probably not much older than I was, maybe in her mid-to-late twenties, but her face looked exhausted and battered beyond her years. Her waist-length auburn hair seemed to be coming loose from some kind of fastening at the back. The pallor of her face was intensified by the deep color of her hair.

She was also very thin, her gown hanging on her, at least a size too big.

I pressed a button to lower my passenger window. "Do you want a ride?"

I didn't really know what I was doing. Something about her made me anxious—my heart started hammering in my chest and I shivered a little, even in the warm night. I had no idea if it was safe inviting her into my car. But she seemed so lost: forlorn, her eyes like broken windows in an abandoned house.

The young woman nodded faintly. A peculiar odor invaded the car when she sat in the passenger seat. It was like two different smells battling each other. One reminded me of a bonfire or wood smoke, a beautiful scent like a forest in autumn; the other a drowning, unclean smell like a swamp, marshy things rotting in polluted soil.

Immediately I regretted the ride, sensing her dank, bleak hopelessness threatening to overpower me. But it was too late. I couldn't tell her to get out—partly from compassion that overrode my fear, and partly from the fear itself. I didn't know who she was. Or what she was.

She looked like a feral creature who'd been raised by wolves.

"Where are you going?" I asked.

She stared me unnervingly in the face. Then she turned to look out through the windshield.

"Away," was all she said. Her voice was hoarse, as if long unused.

"Where—away, where?" I asked, nerves making me stumble over my words. At least I was awake now.

She stared straight out into the night, and seemed to gesture with a faint indent of her head, that away led toward the front gate.

"Okay." I had my hand on the gear shift. "Just tell me when to stop."

As we approached the gate, I heard her take in a ragged breath. Her eyes fixed on its intricate filigreed pattern, the place where the iron bars curved upward, both sides meeting in the middle, the spikes at the top.

As I approached it, the gates slowly opened, and my passenger once again took in an audible breath, clearly in painful suspense, hands clutching the sides of the bucket seat.

"Are you all right?" I asked again.

No answer. But I thought I saw a faint headshake. *No.* I backed up slightly because the iron doors were opening and I'd driven up slightly too close. I put the car in reverse, then stepped on the brake and shifted back into drive.

As I passed through the gate, the first thing I noticed was that the conflicting smells suddenly dissipated, as if sucked out of my car.

I looked over and, to my utter shock and horror, saw nothing. The window was closed, the passenger seat empty.

I stopped the car as the iron doors swung to a slow shutter behind me. I must have sat staring at the empty passenger seat for a full minute. I looked in the back, turning the dome light on. I put the car in park and got out.

The area was still. Not even the normal outdoor sounds—wind rustling leaves, faint animal noises, distant traffic. I feared I'd been sucked into the same void that had swallowed my passenger.

My heart took a wild jagged leap and I scrambled for the front car door. Thankfully, it opened. I got in and clicked all the doors shut. Then I drove like a bat out of hell away from the hospital.

In my driveway, I saw my hands trembling, and I felt queasy, carsick, like I might throw up out of pure fear. When I finally felt ready to face Mom without looking like the shell-shocked survivor of a catastrophe, I gathered my things from the floor. Sitting up, I saw something written on the passenger window.

It was a word written in condensation, but the letters were completely clear.

I scrabbled for my work notebook and wrote the word on it carefully, so I could look it up later to see if it meant anything.

Torschlusspanik.

Later in my bedroom, I typed the strange word into Google. Immediately the translation popped up.

The fear that time is running out and important opportunities are slipping away. Torschlusspanik is a combination of three German words, and literally translated means:

Gate-shut panic.

Victoria

I took it upon myself to look after Miss Owens, who was very aged now, and not long for this world. It broke my heart to see her cast off by her family, even in her final years, dying alone and forgotten in this place.

Miss Owens had been the first person on the ward to listen to my tales of journeying into the future of this asylum, of grotesque and malign medical developments and the practice of unspeakable things on patients. Now, she hung on stories of my recent forays into—the future? My imagination? A parallel universe? I could never fully know. But she listened, enthralled by all these tales of a world that, while still imperfect, was unspeakably more advanced than our own.

As she grew frail, I spent longer hours with her. Finally, she fell and broke her hip, and it was apparent that she had not much longer to live. I sat by her bedside, holding her hand and applying moistened cloths to her forehead.

"Tell me about Doreen," she said in her faint voice.

I smiled. The young woman fascinated me as well. "There has been a new development in her life. She is once again with child. Or so she told the nurse in charge of the ward."

A gasp from Miss Owens. "And still not wed….?"

"No." I smiled ruefully. "Still not wed, and seemingly there is no plan to do so. But the young man responsible for her pregnancies appears to share her life in some way. They also share childcare duties. Though from what I gather, she lives with her mother."

"Who has not disavowed her?"

I shook my head. "No. I gather that her mother also helps her with the child."

Unexpected tears filled her eyes. "Is this a Utopia you have seen, Victoria?"

I smoothed the sparse gray hairs from her forehead. "I do not believe so," I answered. "I cannot understand it all. But I sense there are still contentious issues in the world. In a Utopia, I believe there would be no contention, and no rancor. However, the degree of freedom granted to women—or taken back by women—seems extraordinary." I paused, thinking. "Thusly, if we are in Hell here—" and here Miss Owens nodded agreement with this notion, as vigorously as she could—"perhaps this world I visit might not be Heaven, nor Utopia, but—perhaps a Purgatory?"

She nodded, and the tears sprang into her eyes again. "Do you think—" she began, her voice faltering, as if she barely dared give words to her wish. "Do you think we might go there? After death, or—or in another existence?"

I held her hand tightly, feeling her delicate bones beneath the hot, hectic skin. "Yes, I do, Miss Owens."

"When—when do you think?"

I would have said anything to ease her desperate fear. I did not know the answer to her question. And yet I believed that, since I had been allowed to glimpse this strange new place, then I—and by extension, all of us—might be allowed someday to attain it.

"Soon," I said. "I'm feeling that soon we might go there. Together. We will find ourselves at the gate of that world, and I will hold your hand, and I will lead you into it."

She closed her eyes. Tears trickled out the sides, making thin tracks down her face, which I gently wiped.

She died that night as I held her hand and sat watch over her—the only person on the ward to do so. The nurses sat behind their station, drinking beer and gossiping as she passed.

When they came to take away her body, I felt a desolation I had not experienced at the death of my own father. They were obliged to pry my hand from hers, untangling our fingers by force. They gave me a draught of laudanum and I took it gladly, wanting oblivion, wanting to go to a place where there were no grievous losses. Where human beings were never put away in a warehouse and left to slowly die by decades, abandoned, unloved, and ungrieved by the world.

Mercifully, the opiate in its brandy solvent soon swallowed me whole.

Following Miss Owens' death, I grew ever more determined to make it off the asylum grounds.

On her deathbed, I promised her I would escape, and that I would in some way—even beyond the veil of death—return for her. And it was not only Miss Owens I was seeking to liberate from this prison. It was all the lost girls, the abandoned women, the people thrown away and discarded by the world, the ruined, the destitute, the mad, the melancholy, the nonconforming—all those who did not fit into society's matrix of acceptability.

I did not dwell overmuch on what might happen after I cleared the gate. I suppose that in some wild part of my imagination I hoped that by freeing my spirit of this unholy edifice, I would be freeing my physical body as well. That I would awaken in that world, Doreen's world, and be able to take up my corporeal existence.

Failing that, I dreamed of existing in that time, in the future, even in the astral form I now occupied. I would willingly let my body rot on the asylum ward while I, my essence, went free.

But each time I tried, I smashed up against that wall of impenetrable stone and iron. The gate repelled me, and at that point I would always awaken instantly, into whatever torture chamber I had momentarily escaped.

Doreen

I saw her again on the path. I was always looking now. She turned to me almost eagerly, stopping when I drew up next to her. She put her hand on the passenger door handle, met my eyes through the window. She entered the car when I nodded.

I looked at her as she sat, staring straight ahead, in the front seat. I had the feeling she was building up her courage, or her concentration. Her pale face grew even paler and like before, I saw her hands clench as we approached the entrance to the hospital grounds. From her fearful, determined aspect, I knew she was going to try once again to make it through the gate.

I found myself slowing, and all my muscles tightened. As we approached the entrance, I held my breath along with my passenger, willing her to pass through the gate with me.

Victoria

I tried every way I could imagine to breach that chasm, as wide, it seemed to me, as that between life and death. First Corinthians 13:12 came back to me, echoing in some far corner of my brain:

For now we see but through a glass darkly, but then face to face
Now I know in part, but then shall I know, even as also I am known.

And it seemed to me that fully knowing this strange other time, that I had barely yet had the occasion to explore, might in some way free me.

But the tether remained in place, just as in childhood when I had failed to make my imaginary self turn all the way around.

It finally came to me: I was failing because I kept trying to *force* it.

Once I reached the halfway point, and had turned my astral body to face backwards, which came easy, instead of tightening and digging at myself to make the turn complete, I could loosen my grip. When I tried that, I felt a give, and then in a sort of floating motion I felt myself twist around facing front again.

It was not a complete success. I did not feel as if my whole being turned, but rather my spirit; yet it was at least partially successful, because some fragment of me had accomplished it.

The next time I approached the gate then, either alone or in Doreen's carriage, I resolved to let go of my death grip upon myself, my fierce will to gut my way through the wall; to become lighter instead of denser, to allow whatever force had let me come this far to draw me all the way through.

Doreen

I sensed a difference as soon as she entered the car. She did not look as worn, didn't have her usual jaw-clenched appearance of fear and determination I'd always seen in her. Instead, she seemed to be almost smiling, giving me a glimpse of the pretty young girl she must have been before the asylum ground her down.

Her sense of calm was contagious. Instead of slowing as the entrance loomed ahead, I maintained my speed, holding back just enough to clear the gates.

If I was to be her reverse Charon—ferrying her backward over the River Styx—I knew I had to be steady, grounded. Unafraid.

When the gates started their stately process of giving way, at the moment of passage I glanced at the lady in white, my passenger. Her eyes were open, hands relaxed.

A conviction that I would not see her again came over me, and almost caused me to hesitate; but I knew I could not let her down now. She had trusted me, and she needed me to give her the chance in life I sensed had never been hers. The freedom that I had experienced, that had been denied her, and all others like her in her day.

I didn't even have to ask where she was going. I knew.

Away.

About the Authors

LCW Allingham is an author, editor, and cherished childhood memory. She paints houses for fun and speculates on a daily basis.

Cadence Barrett is a psychotherapist and peer counselor who's worked in numerous psych hospitals, including Norristown State—a modern version of Blackthorn. In her checkered past she's been a police dispatcher, Paris cabaret hostess, and palmist at Fisherman's Wharf. She has two children and a neurotic cat who resists all attempts to be psychoanalyzed.

River Eno is vegan, studies herbalism, the occult, and is the author of the Urban Fantasy novels, "The Anastasia Evolution Series." Her corporeal shell resides on the East Coast in one reality while her brain travels to alternate realities daily.

Melissa D. Sullivan is a writer, editor, parent and semi-professional Tina Fey fan girl. Her writing has appeared in Hippocampus Magazine, Nightingale & Sparrow, Sum Journal and elsewhere and her short story "Dear Jacqueline" was nominated for a 2019 Pushcart Prize. She can often be found in the suburbs of Philadelphia, mourning changes to the Taco Bell menu and plotting out her next strong female lead.

Susan Tulio enjoys writing romances for their optimistic outlook and charm unique to any other form of fiction. She lives near Philadelphia, Pennsylvania, and is currently at work on a new novel.

Acknowledgments

We here at the Writers Block would like to give a huge thank you to designer Adam Allingham for yet another great cover. Capturing the vision of many authors is no small feat and yet you manage again and again.

And to Patricia Allingham Carlson for the use of her beautiful artwork. We thank you from the bottom of our hearts.

Thank you to all who sent us their real-life accounts of a Lady in White sighting. We appreciate your honesty and allowing us to share your stories.

Thank you, also, to author William Donahue who saved us with his brilliant perspectives on horror, and our editor, Di Freeze, who never fails to impress.

A few years ago, LCW. Allingham had an idea for a writing group with a few strange eggs she'd met in other writing groups. There were five of us, and we chose to venture into the world of Utter Speculation because we all respected each other's work, and we enjoyed each other's friendship and support.

Dan Kinter, a kooky and lovable man, had a sense of humor like no other but a no-nonsense approach to writing that helped in times of publishing stress. He was the glue early on, with his "dad joke" sense of humor that could make us roll our eyes and laugh at the same time. He was a grammar stickler and a big pain in our butts, but he was also the propellant to make our first book, *The Lost Colony of Roanoke: A Collection of Utter Speculation,* a reality.

When Dan passed away, shortly after the release of our first book, we struggled to decide if we were enough without him to keep going. Ultimately, we discovered his glue never wore off. The collections of utter speculation are our yearly memorial to a man who gave so much to everyone he met.

We wouldn't be here without you, Dan. We miss you.

Made in the USA
Middletown, DE
22 February 2024